D0457004

Also by the Author

Private Parties (stories)
The Intelligent Traveler's Guide to Chiribosco (novella)
Going Blind (novel)

JONATHAN PENNER

Natural Order

A Novel

POSEIDON PRESS

New York London Toronto Sydney Tokyo Singapore

Poseidon Press
Simon & Schuster Building
Rockefeller Center
1230 Avenue of the Americas
New York, New York 10020

Designed by Karolina Harris
Manufactured in the United States of America

1 3 5 7 9 10 8 6 4 2

Library of Congress Cataloging in Publication Data

Penner, Jonathan
Natural order : a novel / Jonathan Penner.
p. cm.
I. Title.
PS3566.E477N3 1990
813'.54—dc20 90-30828
CIP

ISBN 0-671-66423-9

Permissions on page 171

To Ben

He letteth in, he letteth out to wend,
All that to come into the world desire;
A thousand thousand naked babes attend
About him day and night, which doe require,
That he with fleshly weedes would them attire:
Such as him list, such as eternall fate
Ordained hath, he clothes with sinfull mire,
And sendeth forth to liue in mortall state,
Till they againe returne backe by the hinder gate.

After that they againe returned beene,
They in that Gardin planted be againe;
And grow afresh, as they had neuer seene
Fleshly corruption, nor mortall paine.
Some thousand yeares so doen they there remaine;
And then of him are clad with other hew,
Or sent into the chaungefull world againe,
Till thither they returne, where first they grew:
So like a wheele around they runne from old to newe.

—Edmund Spenser,
stanzas from *The Faerie Queene*

THE CHANGEFUL WORLD

Foulbrood

As a general rule, the beekeeper will not discover it in its incipient stages. He is not expecting it, and if it comes he does not see it. His first intimation of its presence will be occasional cells of sealed brood showing sunken, greasy cappings and cells with irregular perforations. American foulbrood is confined mainly to brood that has died after the cells have been sealed, but from a very few to 75 percent of unsealed cells may show dead brood, and the dead in both sealed and unsealed will vary in color from a yellowish brown to a dark brown, and finally to a brownish black. The larva that has just died holds its shape and lies lengthwise. As the decay advances it begins to shrink, and the dead matter becomes so rotten and putrid that the skin decays and the whole mass flattens down on the under side of the cell.

* * *

One who is expert can very often locate the disease by the odor, but it should be remembered that the odor alone is by no means conclusive. However, in connec-

tion with the other *symptoms the odor is very helpful in enabling one to decide what form of brood disease he has.*

On one occasion the author located a colony having foulbrood by an occasional suspicious odor he could catch at the entrance, but it was nearly a week before he found one cell containing dead matter. Apparently the colony had nearly cured itself, but there still remained a characteristic odor which could not be eliminated. Experience shows that a colony which seems to cure itself does not stay cured. It may be vigorous enough to keep the disease down to some extent. An occasional cell may manifest itself for several years and in the meantime be a constant source of infection to all the rest of the apiary.

—ABC and XYZ of Bee Culture

ONE

In my part of Connecticut—the northeast corner of Fairfield County—you shouldn't get an inch of snow in an April night. But this morning Marigolde's house and lawn are sheeted tight, like things I'm saving that the light might fade.

"Hi," she says, swinging open her door.

I scrape my boots and say, "You need a doormat."

"Don't bother. The carpet's shot." Her deep voice is loud, hoarse.

"From Helen," I say, holding out the fudge.

"She's a love." Marigolde takes it, squeezes and sniffs it. Myself, I don't like surprises, neither giving nor getting them. "Have you had breakfast?"

I try to remember. "Just coffee." She turns, leading the way. Marigolde strides like a man in battle gear, big feet in mannish suede shoes, thickly soled with butterscotch crepe. We cross the living room, whose fleur-de-lis wallpaper I hung so long ago that the time isn't surprising or sad anymore—now the seams are curling and brown—and stand in the little kitchen. When I left, this whole place shrank. She asks me, "Toast?"

Leaning toward her mouth, I'm foolishly happy. Marigolde isn't beautiful, she comes from a time before those words. Before words. Her jaw is primitively large, the widest part of her head. She has big hunting eyes. I imagine going back to her now, today—thoughts that are bad for me.

Her hand goes into my hip pocket. Her long fingers squeeze hard. With the point of her tongue, she wets her lips. I like that: cracked by fine vertical lines, they're always thirsty. "How about," she says, "something to eat."

I say I have to get to work.

"Wait." With knife and forefinger she gives me a square of my wife's fudge, dripping crumbs that I try to catch in mid-air, and takes a square herself. We stand, silently chewing, licking our fingertips.

Then we put on our veils.

Marigolde's back yard falls in terraces toward the river. My hives, forty stacks of white-painted boxes, stand at the lower end, protected from wind by the drop-off of the land. "Better get some boots," I tell her, knowing she won't. Instead she walks in my footprints.

The snowfall worried me, and I'm relieved by the bees' activity. Many are on cleansing flights, staining the snow with brown droppings. Most return with tails high but I can see some hanging bellies, heavy with the early nectar of willows and maples. Marigolde watches, sitting on a stump, hands tucked under her thighs. I heft each hive for weight, then wipe away snow from the entrance. "Thought Eli might be with you," she says. I keep working. Next I know she'll comfort me—she'll tell me all he needs is time. But I believe a paperback I partly read, standing in the supermarket, a book full of confident italics and scornful quotes, which said "your" children aren't "yours" to begin with.

I'm starting the last row when I smell it, fetid as a locker room. In front of one hive, dead grubs dot the snow. As I watch, a bee hauls out another corpse.

I wave her to me and she comes, walking again in my tracks. "Sniff."

"Old meat," she says. "Like meat that's turning."

It takes a couple of minutes to fire up and pump smoke into the hive. When the buzzing softens, I pry out a frame from the brood chamber, shaking off the bees. Then I uncap some cells and dig in a matchstick at what ought to be grubs. I tug out thick goo.

"Poor things," she says. "I'm sorry, Jerry."

But pretty soon, I know, she'll tell me that it doesn't matter. I reassemble the hive and pour calcium cyanide into the entrance. While the gas is killing them I dig the pit. The ground is still hard enough to take a pickaxe, and I'm panting. A helicopter pounds above us, fuselage diagonal to where it's heading, like a dog I once had that walked that way. It slants away toward the Sikorsky plant up-river.

The pit isn't as deep as I want, but I feel weak enough to quit. We dump in the comb-filled frames, the killed bees. Marigolde squirts charcoal lighter and I toss a match. Soon the hive is incinerated, its comb twisted and flowing. I shovel the earth back in. At the first damp thumps, the embers hiss.

When I straighten up I'm dizzy and have to lean on the shovel. "Some coffee," Marigolde says. "Listen, it doesn't matter. Nothing matters. A banana. How about a banana?"

"I'm late," I tell her. "I have to see Woody."

She walks me slowly to my truck, her fingers around my upper arm. "You're sad, donkey. How can I cheer you up?"

"I'm not," I tell her.

"All Eli needs is time."

"I'm happy."

"Sad," she says. "You are." And then I am.

I drive slowly, calmed by sunlight. Heading into the North End, the winding blacktop climbs. White colonial houses. Wide white lawns. The other plate of fudge—for Woody, Helen's brother—is starting to smell good.

Marigolde Small and I come from the other end of Stratford. The South End is reclaimed marshland, streets of identical plywood houses, families too large for them, dented bicycles and wandering dogs. Every class had its Small. In mine, from kindergarten through Stratford High, was Marigolde. Before we ever heard of love, we were facts of one another's lives. So we missed out on the twittery feelings you read about, the sweaty phone conversations you see in movies, that come from not knowing the future. After spending those years in class together, it was an easy change to TV and pillows prickly with popcorn.

We found a house by the river—almost in the North End. That scared and amused her, but made me proud. Soon we met a Yankee gent in flannel shirt and leather suspenders: his family had been original settlers, the Underwoods, and he owned hundreds of acres still. Orchards. Bees. A roadside stand where his son and silent daughter worked. Marigolde and I would stop for apples, cherries, cider, honey.

Exactly why what happened happened, I'm still trying to understand. But it was the Underwoods who changed me, those few minutes I saw them each week. Even less time would have done it, the same way an inoculation, one cloudy half-syringe, can alter you forever. There was no decision involved. I felt myself being led away as though by some bored official.

Marigolde and I began to fight, though I knew she wouldn't change. She brought me expensive presents, not in store boxes, that I was afraid she'd shoplifted. If we made love in the morning, when I came home at night the blankets and sheets would be where we'd flung them. But it wasn't the mess—it was the South End, the way we don't care, we who grew up there. We're happy too quickly, too easily. Marigolde showed me that.

Once, in second grade, a boy had told me that all his family were in a state of grace. I was afraid to ask what that meant. But the phrase, foreign and phosphorescent, remained, so close I sometimes felt it, like the memory of a lost ring. I never felt it when I touched my contented wife.

What did I want? Specifically, what? I went back to school, took classes at night. And there, in the college library, in an aisle that felt as narrow as bedding, I met a woman I'd last seen when she was a girl by the side of the road, weighing out cherries. I looked at her secretly, and she began to smile at the shelf of books in front of her. "I remember you too. I was just a runt," she said. "I had a box behind the counter, and I stood on it whenever you stopped." As she pushed her books across the check-out desk, her fingers' slimness seemed courageous. Outside, we shook hands slowly, with recognition. Now she's been my wife so long our son is half an adult. To Helen, life is a necessary job. To her, it matters what I do, the man I might become.

And early this morning, alone beneath the double quilt, I woke to the smell of fudge. Her humming rose and faded below like the murmur of a swarm. Tiptoeing downstairs—Eli sleeps late, or pretends to—I silently put my arms around her, there in the kitchen's slanting light. I kissed her ear, her black pinned-up hair.

"Jerry," she said, and surrounded herself with something that edged me away.

The Smalls? They're astonished, amazed, by unseasonable weather. Insulted at any rise in the price of gasoline or coffee. They shout advice at game-show contestants, they weep at the outcome of football games. Sometimes so do I—I'm from the South End, too. To South Enders, even ordinary life is outrageous. So our divorce was no big deal.

Immediately, Marigolde was dating men, South End

men her brothers brought home, guys who offered you sticks of gum and didn't button up their shirts. But still I heard "Hi, Jerry!" at the drugstore—her sisters. "Hi, Jerry!" in the five-and-dime. At the liquor store, her father cornered me in the cordials nook, stood sweatily close, and murmured that our wedding picture still stood on Marigolde's dresser.

Her boy friends saw the way it was and never hung around for long. Except one: her second cousin Ken. Loyalty is something Ken can't help. He's loyal to the whole family, every friend he ever had, he's loyal to the South End and loyal to America. But Ken's crude, and his looks are against him. He's too handsome for a regular person. It seems phony, like a movie star portraying a construction worker. The Smalls love him, but his glamour is ridiculous to them. When Marigolde and I were married, I had to feel sorry for Ken, how he'd come up to her so hopefully at family parties. Behind his back, she'd hold her nose until the laughter spun him around. Then she'd hug him like a pet, while a smile of gratitude and lust crept cautiously across his face.

Why should she remarry? If shingles blow off her house, her father, a roofer, replaces them. A brother-in-law mechanic maintains her car. She works for a dentist and knows half of Stratford from phoning patients to remind them of their appointments. She can't be lonely, the Smalls are always getting together, and she can't be bored because for them no experience is over. Everything becomes a story, the far past the same as last night: told and retold, increasingly detailed, fiercely interrupted and corrected.

The gifts! Birthdays, anniversaries, Mother's Day,

Father's Day, Valentine's Day, especially Christmas—they spend forever shopping, asking each other's advice, wrapping presents and hiding them away, opening them with yells and screams of delight. It could make me forget that we'd all grown up. When I was a kid in the South End, our streets blew with gift-wrap paper, metallic green and metallic red, billowing sheets of filmy tissue, streamers of shining silver ribbon, for days into the new year. Even in summer, you might find a scrap of something sparkling, caught in a bush.

Helen doesn't want presents. She doesn't trust what isn't earned. On her birthday, all I do is take her out to dinner at the Venetian Grotto.

It was when old man Underwood died, and I was running the honey business, that I started with Marigolde again. First I moved some hives to her land. After that, when I felt her pulling, I went. And when, lying in bed, she spoke of our getting back together, I wanted that too, though I wondered what to call a man who seemed satisfied only with longing.

Near the top of Deer Hill, hundreds of acres are stripped of cover, carved into streetbeds lined with houses in every stage of construction. Now, noon hour, the hammers are silent. The fat yellow trucks and backhoes, clamshells and graders, each lettered MANGIACAPRA, look abandoned. Men sit in clusters with open lunch boxes. Across Deer Hill Road are the Underwood orchards, and the sign for Deer Hill Farms: PIES & HONEY. PREPARE TO STOP.

His father would have been amazed at how Woody's

developed the business. Apple pies hot from the oven. Peach and rhubarb, lemon chiffon, banana cream, hot from the oven. Now he sells them frozen, too. His non-foods section has Connecticut-shaped ashtrays, mugs with humorous mottos, plaques with humorous mottos, dish towels with humorous mottos, soap resembling fruit, and, filling the whole long room with their scent, row on row of variously colored and shaped bayberry candles. The other room is food: the pies and apples and cider, plus maple syrup and maple fudge, a refrigerated section of expensive cheeses, sourball suckers and horehound candy, saltwater taffy and home-style cookies, and, right beside the register, my tall display of Deer Hill Honey.

"He's not here, Red," the cashier says. My hair is less red than brown and the white is spreading, but Woody calls me that, so his help do too. "He went up to lunch."

"Thanks, Claudia," I say. She doesn't catch it, and makes inquiring eyes—her machine is totaling with an electronic beep. I wave to show I understood. In the line of customers waiting to pay, nobody's buying honey. I check my stock: stacks of one-pound bottles, two-pound bottles. Cellophane-wrapped comb honey. Then I see that next to my display, touching it in fact, is a smaller one, a few bottles, a few sections of comb. I grab a bottle—Uncle Seth's Pure Organic—and head out, and starting from the skin of my palm I'm angry.

Woody and Violet have a stone-and-glass split-level designed by a Boston architect. As soon as I ring the two-tone chimes the dogs begin to bark.

"Red." Woody sweeps back a hand. Then he sees the fudge. "You shouldn't've done that. Shut up!" The dogs, confined in a distant room, stop barking instantly. He turns off the sound on the TV, where a gymnast has her legs in an impossible position. "Vi!"

I show him the bottle. "Who's Uncle Seth?"

Woody's face gets sober. Though he never takes a vacation, he's tan from the sunlamp at his health club. He lifts weights three nights a week, and his forearms, bare below rolled-up sleeves, are twice the size of mine. "Red," he says gently, "there's some things we need to get together on."

Violet enters, her smile crazily wide, as though she's about to brush her teeth. When she sees me, her cheeks relax. "Hello, Jerry. I thought you were Mr. Mangiacapra. Wasn't he coming back?"

"He was just here," Woody tells me. "The little—" He stops himself from saying some word, like wop or dago. Those are South End words. North Enders don't use them, if they remember. "Pastafazool," he says.

I ask what he wanted, but I know. Mangiacapra is ready for our side of the road, now. He's already made one offer that Woody claims to have laughed at. Woody shakes his head. "I wonder what he pays for his suits."

"What'd you tell him?" Woody doesn't know that Mangiacapra has come to me too. We haven't talked figures, but he's made me dream. Winking, he said he wouldn't mention our conversation to anyone, and I hated him for knowing me so easily.

"What do you think?" Woody says. "Kicked him out."

"Jerry," says Violet, turning her smooth face, "I'm fixing lunch."

I tell her Helen's expecting me, and follow Woody to his pine-paneled den. On one wall are massively framed photographs, studio portraits with no shadows, of hunting dogs he's owned. His gun cabinet stands opposite. Centered on his desk, two bottles of honey: Deer Hill and Uncle Seth's Pure Organic.

"Fellow came by," he says, a little sadly. "Very nice fellow. Just started a bee yard in Fairfield. I said I'd take a few on a one-shot basis, just to see what he's got. Now, Red, look at this label."

"Cute." The bee in farmer's overalls is nothing I'd put on a product of mine. "How's it taste?"

"And look." Woody goes to the window. In sunlight, the hair at the top of his head is so delicate I want to protect it with my hands—he's having it transplanted from the back of his neck. Dramatically, he raises both bottles. My honey looks dark, the other golden.

"Woody, for God's sake, that's the shape of the container." Mine's a cylinder. Uncle Seth's is a flat oval. "That's just daylight coming through."

"Your customer doesn't know that. Count on it, this guy is visiting every one of your outlets. He hasn't got much production now. But wait a year and he'll emasculate your marketing."

"How's it taste?"

He uncaps Uncle Seth and we dip in fingers. "Sort of thin," he says, sucking. He's being kind; he knows better. "Lots of clover," I tell him. "Good clover in there."

"Here's another item he's doing." He hands it to me: one of those plastic squeeze bottles, a honey-filled buck-toothed bunny, upright on its haunches. Erect ears form the spout. I hand it back.

"All read-y," Violet sings.

Woody sighs, but I know he hasn't quit. "Look," he says. "Tell Helen you're eating with us. There's a lot more we need to discuss." And he takes my elbow, guides me toward the phone. "Okay? We'll eat. Want a beer? We'll eat and we'll talk."

Except for the forty that Marigolde has, and the nursery colonies near my house, all my hives are in Woody's orchards: four hundred in clusters of twenty. Full of beer and food and advice, I'll do as many as I can in what's left of the afternoon. The clouds are pumped fat with rain. Tomorrow the bees may not fly.

When I come to the stand of hives that Eli's supposed to take care of, I try not to watch too long, guessing the yield from the traffic. I've decided my son hates bees, unless it's me he hates—I swear he holds his breath every time I walk by. His problem is more than me, though. Nothing's good enough for him. He's enrolled at the community college, but he goes there and comes home in a dream. Helen thinks there's something unwholesome going on with one of his teachers.

I say I'm from the South End, that's what I tell people. But if they knew how I worry about my kid, they wouldn't believe it, and they'd be right. I moved there when I was eight. So I never learned that families are inexhaustible, and time will wait, and anything that happens is probably okay.

I came with my father, after my mother died. He'd heard of a job at Stratford Plating. Every night, taking off my clothes, I still see my father's back, its design of cotton-white patches, which I painted with salve before he went to sleep. Each year the chemicals engraved him deeper as he worked, shirtless, lowering racks into bubbling tubs. Now I take care of his grave, and after I'm gone, Helen will do it. She didn't like my father, he didn't like her, but she'll do it because he's under there and the grass is growing and no one else will care.

By the time I come to the next stand I know from my ears, the way they're beginning to burn, that the temperature is falling. I move down the rows, hefting the hives, resettling them so the rain will drain out. Once I'm stung, feel the give of the bee's body an instant before the pain. With my pocketknife I scrape the shaft from the ball of my thumb.

Here, beyond Woody's west boundary, lies the new high school—people still call it new. The hives are in sight of the parking lot, where motorcyclists gather in the evening, gunning their engines, drinking wine and smashing bottles. I've seen them roar onto the baseball field, racing by headlight, spinning and rearing, gouging wallows into the grass and base paths.

Already, the day is silting up, darkness rising from the earth. The apple trees stretch toward the light like seaweed. I think of our four-poster bed, where both Helen's parents died. Along my side, where in a few hours she'll be lying, I feel her now.

These are the times I like best. When I'm tired from work, out in the orchards. It's the bees, with their patterns and seasons, who live in grace. For them the world is perfect by accident. For me, that accident takes so much design, such planning and waiting.

I've almost reached my truck when I see a dark spot move on the snow. I crouch for her: a nearly frozen worker. By her dullness, the raggedness of her wings, she's old, a survivor from last fall. Most of her generation are dead.

I hold her, still crouching in the snow, warming her in my hand. *Huh huh huh*—I breathe on her. Soon she begins to crawl on my palm, climbs to the tip of my forefinger. She clings there, buzzing her wings. In just another moment, she'll be gone.

T W O

Eli carried the three blue-and-gold dinner plates from the kitchen cabinet to the dining room. Passing behind his mother, who was stirring a steaming saucepan, he held his breath. You couldn't tell when you were inhaling her. She smelled of nothing, except, faintly, the washing machine—the way it smelled right after it stopped and you opened its dripping door.

The news, he imagined, would come from Uncle Woody. The phone would ring in its normal manner. *Listen calmly. You're going to have to tell your mother.* And Marigolde: the cow would come over (wild tears). Doctor, mortician, lawyer. *I assume you know that everything is yours. Your mother can live in the house as long as she doesn't remarry.*

He positioned the plates. Eli knew where things should go and preferred to set the table himself. He also liked to be the one who slid the t. p. onto its roller—his mother sometimes loaded it to unwind brutally from the front. If he didn't close the Venetian blinds, he'd have to walk around reversing the ones that his father had closed with convex sides inward.

In the kitchen, his mother was turning plump lumps of frying chicken. Eli started to arrange the spoons and forks, napkins and knives. A thud was followed by a crash. Dizzy, he rushed in: Mom! Leaning over the dining-room table, he felt his lips shape the word. Sit her up, remove shoes, loosen her clothing—his panic swelled. His mother's dead body, the thought of it, scared him in a way his father's didn't. From forgotten baths, he remembered just her patch of black hair, thickly curled, holding bubbles of air that rose in a sudden spray when she brushed it.

Car crash, the officer said heavily, and Eli nodded, seeing his father's severed limbs, head rolling on the floor mat. The air was pink from the blood across the windows. *He always had these dizzy spells.* Though his father said they were nothing, even fat Marigolde had come to talk to Eli's mother about them—Aunt Marigolde, she wanted him to call her. After his father's death, she wouldn't enter this house again. *You had him enough years,* Eli told her, but while she was gasping for an answer drew back his words to say instead, *You've had enough of him,* and then rewrote his line once more: *You had your chance, and now he's dead.*

Years ago, riding on the bus, he'd seen his father's truck pull alongside with her in the passenger's seat. Eli had looked away instantly, as though he'd opened the door on them naked. He felt he'd shamed his father by seeing them, himself unseen. They weren't touching. But when the truck jounced they swayed together, her skirt above her knees. They'd stayed alongside for blocks.

Eli looked once more—his father's hand, with tapping fingers, still rode the gearshift knob—before the bus slowed for a stop. After that, he had felt afraid whenever his father mentioned Marigolde. It was something he should never have seen.

Glasses. In the kitchen, his mother was lowering a frozen block of spinach into boiling water, leaning backward to keep her face out of the steam. She asked how school— "Fine," he said.

"Are you enjoying your teachers?"

He turned away to carry the glasses into the dining room. VV was who she meant. "Please come back," his mother called.

He said softly, "Leave me alone."

"Please come here a moment."

Her casualness warned him—"moment" instead of "minute." He stood in the doorway, arms folded, while she wiped her eyeglasses on her apron. As she frowned to bring him into focus, her eyes looked as if they hurt. "You've gotten stuck. Something's happened, hasn't it. You're immobilized."

"Everyone alive is stuck," he said. Then, when he saw her turn away, replacing her eyeglasses on her nose, he told her, "You don't have to worry."

"Don't patronize me, Eli." She lowered the flame under the chicken. "Will you please put out the bread and things?" she asked, with a formality that saddened him.

"Okay. And don't you patronize *me.*"

By now his father was usually home. The house was waiting for him. Eli felt it: the wood floors and faded Oriental rugs, lumpy sofa and threadworn chairs, the blackened fireplace, the old TV. Every night they

awaited his father. Th
its upward-marching d
mantelpiece. Each pa
Eli walked from room
He knew every cra
squeal in the floorboa
his. Once they had
this memory (which
wasn't a fact) fright
see that lost house
ergreens in front.
clearer and clearer
rain spout, welco
mailbox sprouted
searched for the h
somewhere near
Bent over the
the big looselea
tabs, that she u
He wanted to
clothes to cha
in her lap. H
of sherry. He
once talked,
Instead he as
"He'll be
there some
Eli return
had been che
BRAKES FAI
uaries: Jerr

family
ith cold
ngs amaze
nk, rubbin
f wax, he s
a bee visit
retty—"
hem. "But *the*
tions, Eli could
aking the spin-
is mother, too,
food. Their in-
e'd seen it the
s so fastidious,"
ook care of his
n?"
er, "went over
VV had been
food, his father
e noticed you're
Eli: *You're the*
e are capable of
d her desk and

w. She stroked his tem-
ith her fingernails, until
ing his head against her
his pantsleg. *Your mind*
play chess? Suddenly he
at the ceiling, and his
is knife and fork were
at. The chess club: she
n.
oday," his father said
ld, as though he were
i's hives. Occurred to
fairly soon." Eli said
bout an illustration in
ly enlarged, precisely
ly disgusting mouth
and worked and died
r mortality, sickened
ell me about school
t was so interesting:
herds packing the
e of class with an
"
aid ironically. "Be-
ing well at all."
ew things too good
ointed him—their
bvious and few—
ew he was luckier
mply fools. Violet

screeched at her big TV, watching other fools win prizes of merchandise. Woody sold signs in his store that said

Eli was patriotic himself—at night, waiting to fall asleep, he'd twitch at the *whump-whump-whump* of bullets, interposing his body to save the President from assassination. He didn't believe his uncle would sacrifice a fingernail.

"Woody thinks," his father said, "we're not doing all we could." Then they discussed Woody's advice. Jars, prices, outlets, advertising—they took it as seriously as quicksand. *It's perfectly plain,* VV said, over coffee in the cafeteria, or in her kitchen (he imagined it high in some apartment building), where she'd invited him to talk—they'd never really had a chance, had they—*it's perfectly obvious that you're more advanced than the other students.* There was a rumor that she had cancer. Some days her voice was weak and she looked like she'd been bled before class. *More advanced spiritually, if I can, I mean may, if I may use that word.* Eli frowned in thought: *How do you mean?* Her eyes seemed to swell with significance. *You are aware of possibilities.* "Sixty-pound cans," his father said. "A dime more than wholesale." She leaned forward and kissed him. From her bedroom window, you could see Long Island Sound. Eli told her not to close the curtains.

"A dollar a pound over cost, Woody estimates," said his father. "And that includes shipping."

He finished his food quickly. That these thoughts were nothing, would come to nothing, was fine. But why were they attending him? Eli wasn't concerned with sex—not the way overage virgin boys pretended to be in movies. Last summer he'd emptied his bank account and taken the train to New York City. Outside the station, a hairy person had handed him a leaflet describing a place of total personal service—a place to savor utter relaxation—an oasis of ultimate delight. And this language, he slowly understood, reading it over as he walked repeatedly west and east on a block of 42nd Street, was enough. Here in his hand, free and safe, already memorized, was the illusion of knowledge for which he had come.

"I don't want any more," he said. "It was good, Mom." He couldn't remember tasting anything. "I guess I'm going up now."

His parents both looked at him, smiling with love. He knew that his tone of voice had pierced them, thrown them back to his childhood. They loved him. They still did. That was wonderful. But there was something peculiar about it, too.

• • •

I DON'T KNOW WHO I AM. I DON'T KNOW WHAT I AM. I DON'T KNOW WHAT I'M PART OF. He leaned forward, reading and rereading the three sentences.

His room was dim. One of the bulbs in his ceiling light was dead. On the floor beside his desk, wrapped in its cord, lay a study lamp, a hopeful present from his parents. He'd had to tell them he couldn't use it. Its fluorescent hum seemed to be inside his head. Downstairs they were talking. He could hear the ring of dishes being scraped, and then the gush and rumble of the dishwasher.

Eli read the sentences again. He didn't know what else to say, or whether he could read even this aloud to a roomful of people. At first, when VV copied the classified ad on the board—an item she'd noticed in the paper—it had seemed like something he would never consider.

Reincarnation study group to
meet weekly. 324-6110

Study group sounded stupid, and reincarnation had never interested him. Why hadn't it?

SO REINCARNATION

He crossed out the first word. Then he crossed out the second and immediately rewrote it.

REINCARNATION

She hadn't said they should go, or that she was going herself. But Eli guessed she was, she had to be. All she'd said was something he hadn't followed—he was watching the way she made her eyes get solemn—about challenges and assumptions. Then he'd gotten hard, and when he crossed his legs she smiled. It was later, at home, that he'd realized the subject was remarkable. If it were true, that would change everything. There were probably scientists at work on it right now. The government would have to be interested. The strategic implications were enormous.

This must be kept absolutely secret. The President's voice was soft, husky, his speech slow—he was an old, old man. *If the world ever found out, human society as we know it, as we know it*

REINCARNATION MIGHT EXPLAIN

But how could he say, among strangers, everything it might explain? Finally he'd called the number in the advertisement. The phone had been answered on the first ring. "This is Cyril," a warm baritone voice announced.

Eli had nearly hung up. But the voice was so assured. "I was calling," he explained—his own voice thin and pathetic, his face hot, as though he were speaking into an oven—"about, you know. The ad." There was no response. "The meeting," he said more firmly.

"Reincarnation?" The matter-of-factness of the question implied that this was a normal phone call, and Eli was grateful for that. "First I'd like to know about you."

Eli gave his name, his age, and said he was a freshman in college. He felt there was much more to tell, but Cyril said, "That's all I need. You aren't a phony, Eli. If we feel profound respect for life, technique will follow. We'll start with the basics. Students who can accept reincarnation, who'll buy it as a working idea—are you with me?"

"Yeah, as a working—"

"—will embark on a fascinating adventure. I require a written statement explaining your interest in the subject. We'll read them aloud. You'll meet businessmen, professionals, people of this caliber." The last vague category included professors, Eli was sure. Would she smile when she saw him? He smiled back, into the phone. But after he had hung up, his excitement seemed greedy. If VV had cancer, reincarnation would be far more important to her than it was to him.

Requiring a statement was a test, he realized, now that he was trying to write it. Explaining what he felt—making it not seem silly—appeared to be impossible.

REINCARNATION MIGHT EXPLAIN

why it wasn't his, this life. He even looked as if he didn't belong here. Shorter than both his parents, sharper-featured: someone had grabbed the tip of his nose and pulled. He'd seen, with two mirrors, how a quarter inch of septum showed pink beneath an arc of nostril. His father was square-chinned, his mother long-chinned. Why was his—he fingered it—cleft like an apple of bone?

The Russians, said the President, softly, huskily, very slowly, *the Russians and the Japanese must not get hold of this. Our national survival.*

A spotlight rose on the Director, seated opposite him. His voice grated. *They're already working on it.*

What's our lead?

The Director shrugged. *A year. Six months. Then they'll launch a first strike. That's our analysis. Soon as they know they'll live again, no matter what we hit them with.*

Death. The President spoke more softly than ever. *The idea of death. That's all that's protected us. I mean the, you know, the illusion of it.*

A fly buzzed at the ceiling fixture. How could there be such big ones so early in the year? It seemed weak—old or sick. Eli watched it drop to the floor, buzz there, manage to lift off again, and land on his pad of paper. He struck to kill and was horrified by the smudge of black guts. Then he saw it was only ink. He'd swung with his fountain pen in his hand.

REINCARNATION

What would be really interesting would be if some reporter learned what the government was doing. Eli himself would never leak it. But he could imagine how it would look, the first news story—brief, because little would yet be known, its full importance not realized—but certainly on the front page. And definitely in a box.

He turned to a clean sheet of his notepad, unzipping his pants to let his prick stand free while he wrote. He let it warm one hand. Triple-spacing to leave room for revisions, he started the first draft, leading his story out, turning and sculpting it, bringing it toward its perfect form, the way he needed it, the way VV, he hoped, would wish it to be.

When he finished, it was late. He got into his pajamas, went to the bathroom, brushed and flossed his teeth. Then he stood at his desk, reading through what he had written.

He turned out the lights and slid into bed. Outside, the wind was moaning in the apple trees. He heard his father and mother come up, heard them use the bath-room, first her, then him. "Good night," he called, as he did every night, and they called back, "Good night." Then the door of their room closed, and he heard their bedsprings groan.

Eyes wide open, he lay waiting for sleep. The wind moaned louder. It came into Eli's mind how wrong his father was—it was terrible to live in the middle of nature. It was gruesome. Macabre was what it was. The nuts and apples fell, flowers bloomed and withered, leaves fell and lay decaying, birds mated and laid their eggs and the eggs hatched and the birds died, shells of dead beetles lay in the troughs of windowsills. All around you, things were rushing toward death at a pace faster than the human. Whenever he thought this way he made himself think instead of the sea, which never changed. Though of course the sea had creatures in it too, hidden under the water, dying and teeming and dying.

THREE

"Warning," said Jerry Hook. "This honey is not—"

The house shook in a blast of wind. It seeped through the window frames. The bedroom curtains, hanging in the dark as though they'd been executed, swayed helplessly. But the rain still hadn't come, and Hook tried to stop listening for it.

Palumbo's Italian Supply had complained about his honey hardening. Add a heating stage, Woody had said, increase your shelf life. Hook thought heating killed the taste. He preferred an explanatory label.

"Is." Lying in the curve of his body, Helen whispered over her shoulder. "Say what it is. Say what it does."

The house gave off pops and cracks, like casual gunfire far away. Somewhere water was circulating with a confidential hiss. Hook placed it in the upstairs toilet. Leaking drain seal. Hardware store tomorrow.

His lips against Helen's hair, his knees tucked into the open angles of hers, he stroked her side from long-fingered ribcage to crest of hip. Under his hand, her thin nightgown bunched and caught. "I think I'm getting my period," she said, rolling away from him onto her stomach. "Rub my back?"

He hitched closer, over the warmed spot where she had been, and began to massage the back of her thin neck, then down between her shoulder blades, circling each knuckle of spine. Into the narrow of her back, up the bony slope below, to the dimple that became a cleft. If he went beyond, she'd tighten. He rubbed her back and squeezed. "That's wonderful," she murmured. If he touched her mostly here, she'd let his hand wander out to the point of her shoulder and return along her side, fingertips slow on the edge of her breast.

"It may granulate," she whispered. "Say what it may do."

Hook thought her elegant. Helen could have modeled underwear for magazines, posed on a pearl-gray page, or hip-to-hip with other narrow women in a catalogue. By contrast Marigolde was awkward, thick as an umpire. Hook couldn't guess why he loved her more, even to the black hairs on her breasts, or why he wished he were married to her again.

And so he might be. A situation was made of components. The first was to straighten Eli out, but that was imaginable: Eli joyous, laughing on the phone with a girl; Eli serious, studying late, a line of light below his bedroom door. Next, fold the honey business. He'd sell his land to Mangiacapra. Hook felt the pen between his hurrying fingers as he endorsed the check over to Helen. After that he'd be free, living with Marigolde, in their old home by the river. Hook was practical, he believed. Regardless of all his irregular thoughts, his firm ideas were of things that could happen.

"May granulate," Helen murmured, "during storage."

"Lengthy storage," Hook said. "Goodness is unaffected. To reliquefy, place jar in hot water." Moments when the wind fell, he heard a distant rush like the sound inside a revolving door—cars on the Merritt Parkway—and, drifting from miles farther, where the Connecticut Turnpike bridged the Housatonic, the rumbling hum of trucks.

He pressed closer, rubbing Helen's back harder, until she sighed "Wonderful" and rolled against him, her back touching his front everywhere, the cold bottoms of her feet resting on the warm tops of his. "I know I'm getting my period," she said.

He lay with his arm around her, his hand now stroking her neck and parts of her breasts—she didn't like him to touch her long nipples. She slid a hand up his pajama sleeve to smooth his wrist and forearm. Hook waited for a response in himself. No matter how he touched her, she'd catch her excitement only from his, which would come, if it came at all, from nowhere, a forgotten name. He lowered his hand to her flat stomach. He traced the grooves where her long legs joined her body. "This is on my mind," she said. Then she asked Hook whether he knew what they'd cleared last year. Net profit.

The room was so dark that the ceiling could have been miles above. Talk of money felt to him like talk of a death still distant but certain. It was a North End disease. In the South End, money had been a knowing joke, like big breasts in cartoons—you desired, caught yourself desiring, and laughed. His hand continued to stroke Helen for a minute after he wanted to stop. Hook feared he didn't understand anything human, like money or love, the same way other people did. He trusted appearances too much. He told a tree's health from its leaves, he knew the condition of a colony of bees by cocking an ear, by the smell of the hive or its weight. All he was sure he could judge was disease.

When he didn't answer she told him the bottom line, less even than he'd guessed.

Helen did the books, wrote the checks, sold to stores. She'd gotten the A&P to stock their honey, the Safeway, the Grand Union. Hook had known and told her that it wouldn't work: not with the store brand right alongside, twenty cents cheaper. The business mistakes were hers, but he couldn't say so. Helen had no lover, no other life waiting as Marigolde was waiting for him. All she had was Deer Hill Honey. Even her father's life insurance had gone into the business. Hook thought of Marigolde alone in her bed, her heavy soft body. He remembered her scent and curled himself like paper held toward fire.

"Marketing's changed," he said. "There's money in mail order. You advertise in magazines, little ads, back in the classifieds."

"Where people look for sex partners."

"Store prices. Shipping included."

"Sincere male, thirty, seeks—seeks—"

"Direct from the bee to you."

"Fiftyish gal with zest for life—"

"Come on. Where do you see those things?"

"There's paperwork, there's packing. Mail order isn't simple."

"Try bulk," said Hook. "Restaurants. Bakeries."

"No, you can't haul sixty-pound cans."

"I could if Eli would help me." Then he was sorry he'd spoken the name.

"Jerry, tonight he gave me such a shitty feeling."

Once he'd wanted many children—that way, you could afford to feel anything about them. For the Smalls, kids were entertainment, and whatever you felt was only emotional exercise, a healthy workout. Having just one was different. It made Hook nervous to discuss him. Eli was like a fire so low it might go out if you breathed too close. "It's okay," Hook said. "He's all right. He just needs time."

"I have an awful feeling about that teacher. Maybe you should go over to the college."

She stirred in the dark, kneeing the bedding violently—drafts of cold air were sucked in, making Hook shiver. Helen was tugging on her sleeping socks. "I'm worn out," she said. She found his hand and squeezed it. "I hope you don't mind."

"Of course not," he said automatically.

"Good night, darling." She rolled away from him.

"Good night," he said, "sleep well," and rolled toward his own side of the bed, drawing his feet up from the chill of the sheets. He didn't much care. He was tired himself. But because he'd expected to, and because he'd been thinking of Marigolde, he knew it would be hard to fall asleep without making love.

In the old oak on the north side of the house, branches were rubbing each other in the wind. Hook imagined a snapped bough, not quite severed, tossing and sawing like a violinist's bow, and wondered whether he could reach it with his pruning saw. He thought of his land, how deep it went—four thousand miles, he supposed, narrowing to a dot at the center of the earth. And even down there, on three sides of him, like a puzzle piece embracing a smaller piece, was Woody's land. Tonight its surface, curling with apple orchard, would be wind-tossed like the hair of teenagers dancing. The oak tree groaned. Helen turned, reshaping her pillow.

It wasn't just the clasp of her brother's land—it was Woody himself who made Hook feel surrounded. Where Hook floundered, Woody had plans, updated annually on his birthday. Once, to encourage Hook, to show him what he too ought to be doing, Woody had brought out a leather-bound diary with sections for one-year, five-year, and lifetime goals. Hook had been impressed. There were business targets—value of plant, annual gross, number of employees. In his early fifties, he'd go public and diversify, stay on as corporation president. But only briefly: by fifty-five he planned to run for State Senate, serve two terms, and then campaign for governor. He'd finally thrown into the fire a similar book he'd started for Pal, a kid who—admit it, admit it—was headed nowhere unless it was prison. But you, Red, he told Hook, thumping the notebook with his fist, *you* should've been going by one of these, all these years.

Helen was breathing deeply, still on her back, which meant awake. The house shook in the wind as though it had been kicked. The television antenna whirred, sending a hum down its mooring wires into the timbers of roof and walls. The antenna would hold, Hook knew. He'd driven in the bolts himself. His beehives would be rocking on their bases, but too heavy with honey, he thought, to fall before anything less than a hurricane.

She half sat up in bed, punched her pillow, and sank

back into it. "Can't sleep?" Hook asked. He rolled toward her and she met him in the middle of the bed. It was the moment before they touched, as they were reaching for each other, that a circuit closed and desire ran through him.

They lay with their arms around each other, one of her warm legs bent at the knee and clasped between his. He pressed himself against her, stroking her, whispering in her ear that he loved her. Helen's hand slid between the buttons of his pajama top, slowly down and up his side. Her thumbnail rose along the edge of his belly and chest, scraping lazily across a nipple. His erection, pressed between them, felt foreign against his stomach. He stroked the backs of her thighs, and then, reaching between them, the sticky lips of her vagina. After a minute she grabbed his hand.

Hook struggled out of his pajamas. Helen reached down to tug off her socks, pulled her nightgown over her head, her body turning in the dark like a fish far down in the water.

They were silent as he guided himself into her. The wind had fallen; the long shriek of a train whistle floated from the south. He worked his hands under her. She chorded his back like a keyboard. Only the pressure of her fingers and the rhythm of her breath told him what she wanted, and he was often in doubt. Marigolde, with her hoarse whispers, was clear as a manual, and when she came, you knew. Hook had never been certain that Helen came at all, but had always understood that she didn't want to discuss it. He kicked away the tangled bedding. *To reliquefy,* he thought, *place jar in hot water. Honey will still have all its goodness.* His orgasm rose and he stopped in time. "Come on top?"

She shook her head, laced her fingers through his hair, kneading the back of his skull. "Mangiacapra was here today," she said. "He was looking for you."

Hook held himself still. "What did he—"

"He didn't say." She began to move beneath him, a short motion, a careful angle that inflamed him. "He gave me a shitty feeling too. Anyone can see what he wants."

Hook could see it. The developer wanted his land as a lever to pry out Woody, who fronted Deer Hill Road from the reservoir to the nature preserve. Hook kneed Helen's legs farther apart as he thrust. Her hands began to move aimlessly. Now his mind withdrew to contemplate his pleasure, as though memory could conserve it—how this felt, and this. He would sell, he thought without interest. It was nothing he could pay attention to now, but he would go to Mangiacapra's office and sell him the land. His balls slapping against his wife, he came, turning his head away, pressing his face into the pillow.

Things returned: the pillow, Helen's chest against his, the tiredness in his hands, still under her. In a minute he would have to get up. After he came, she couldn't keep him inside. He had never understood this; he and Marigolde would fall asleep that way. Helen moved a knee, her signal. Hook withdrew carefully, as though he were pulling a splinter.

She handed him tissues from the box she kept beside the bed, and he wiped himself while she went into the bathroom. He was startled awake when the bed shifted as she got back in. "That was wonderful," he told her.

"I have my period," she said. She stroked his arm.

"You brought it on." And Hook felt as pleased as though he really were part of that cycle, grateful for the sap already drying on him. In the morning it would be crusty and pink, as though he had bled too.

"Good night," she whispered. With an effort, he leaned over and kissed her on the mouth. As he fell back onto his pillow he was already groggy. Far away he heard the drone of a motorcycle, and thought of his hives being visited, vandalized. But Hook was too happy for worry. He realized that if he were told this moment that he was about to die, he could listen with only the vaguest regret. As he heard, rattling his window, the first pellets of the rain he'd been expecting, he fell gradually asleep, feeling as sticky as honey, as torpid as honey, as full of sweetness, as translucent.

F O U R

"There's ice cream," my mother says, "it's chocolate," so I go into the kitchen to spoon it out. If I let my father serve, there'll be brown smears on the bowls. If she does, it will come to the table in terrible little balls.

What's on the agenda, he'll ask me. Which is unfair, because he knows I'll tell. To me, lying is like growing a beard, or like the movies, with a theater full of hypnotized rabbits. I don't go to movies. Not anymore.

I carry in the three bowls. The lights flicker—it's been storming all day. Then the phone rings and it's Pal. His father won't give him the car.

"God damn him," he says. "God *damn* him."

It's strange about relatives—whether they're any good doesn't matter. Your cousin, everyone said, your only cousin. Pal frightened me: his dragon books and monster toys, the stuffed lion that he told me ate his enemies. But they talked me into loving him when I was too young to decide such things. Now he's like a book report I wrote when I was in third grade—it's been in my desk drawer so long that I'd feel rotten if I threw it away.

Besides, when we were in junior high, I got "Cutest Smile" in the yearbook. All Pal got was "King of the Jungle(?)." I'll have to spend the rest of our lives showing that I'm on his side.

"It's okay," I tell him. "I'll ask."

"I'll just take ours," he says.

You will like hell, I hear Woody shout.

"It's my goddamn *car*!" Pal yells, right into the phone. I pull it away from my ear and my parents look at each other.

With Pal it's always the same. I used to watch while he let the air out of people's tires. I watched him paint EAT THE HAIRY BIRD on the boys' room mirror. One night I watched him squat and crap on the front steps of his father's store. There's nothing he can do about himself. He still thinks he's king of the jungle. If we walk down the hall behind a pretty ass, I have to hold him up by the collar. Otherwise he'll start collapsing, making awful squeaks and grunts, into the swinging, knuckle-dragging waddle of a gorilla. When we play chess, he calls himself the Rajah, but if I'm winning he'll say his pieces are torpedoes and start launching them with a flick of his forefinger, knocking mine over. He makes me sit in his bedroom and listen for hours to crimes that are sure to work. Kidnapings, hijackings, clever murders. When we hear his father come home—the dogs begin to bark—he raises his middle finger toward his closed and locked door.

When I mentioned reincarnation, naturally he laughed. He said just what I expected: "You must be hot as hell for her." And after the meeting he'll be sarcastic, I know. I'm used to his personality. But with Pal it isn't personality—it's an automatic physical thing, like sweating or sneezing. I tell him I'll call him back.

It's my belief that someday you'll be able to go into Bridgeport instantaneously. They'll find ways to transmit matter in electromagnetic waves. You'll go along wires or through the air, like sunlight. My parents are looking at me. "Pal can't get the car," I say. "Can I take ours?"

"What's on the agenda?"

"We're going out."

He nods, and next it's her turn. They're doubles partners, taking turns at the net. "What's up tonight?"

"I'll tell you," I say. "Are either of you interested in reincarnation?"

She smiles, not happily, and he says, "I don't think so." I explain that some people are getting together to talk about it. I don't mention VV since that would confuse the issue. My mother already thinks I'm sleeping with her. That's why she asks me now at whose house this will be. And my father says, "Reincarnation?", looking like the milk for his coffee is sour. "I don't believe in that. Just make this life as good as you can."

"He'll learn through experience," she says, as if I want to do something stupid but harmless.

I tell them, "Thanks for being so understanding." He says not to be a wise guy, and she asks again where it is. "Cyril, is the guy's name. His house. It was in the paper."

"Last name?"

"I didn't ask."

He's shaking his head. "How do you know this is legitimate?"

I tell them maybe it isn't, I'll find out when I get there.

And finally she says to have fun, I can go. "Is there a phone number?"

I show them and he copies it down. "Have fun," he says too. Fun: that's what they want for me. "Drive extra carefully. The streets are wet."

"The truck?"

"The Beetle."

"Please look out for yourself," she says. Then, when I see the expression in their eyes as they stand there watching me, like I'm too precious to take a chance with, I want to stay home.

GENERAL INTRODUCTION

1. Welcome to the elite. Kahlil Gibran, Plato, Wordsworth, Benjamin Franklin, Frederick the Great, Mohandas K. Gandhi, Henry David Thoreau, and Henry Ford all accepted the truth of reincarnation.

What a coincidence, says VV, laughing. But then she says she thought I'd be here. She sits opposite me in trousers, legs crossed, so I can't help looking. I imagine sleeping with her and seeing that she does have cancer—feeling it before I see it—a wet red pit in her side. There's VV, me, Cyril, Pal. A long-haired girl in a poncho didn't have the two dollars. The man in soft goods, maybe my father's age, paid it for her. There's a younger guy, bearded, who's studying divinity, and a geezer with leaflets about the right to life. He distributes them from a slipping armful.

I hope the Volks will be okay outside. It's a poor neighborhood—closed factories, peeling warehouses, blocks of shabby double houses. These are tall and pointy-roofed and thin, as if they had to inhale to squeeze into their lots. Cyril's half of one is a second-floor apartment.

When we're all sitting around and I'm wondering when something official will happen, he says, "I was afraid nobody would come. Companionship and love are the same as reincarnation. Love accomplishes in the infinite width of a single moment what reincarnation does in the infinite length of all moments. Simultaneous and serial. One guards us against despair and the other against death. Synchronic and diachronic. I have here a general introduction." He distributes photocopies that smell faintly burned. "But before we begin anything else," he tells us, "follow me."

Cyril gets up. Thick everywhere—body, arms, neck—and it moves like all of it's muscle. Skin white as a toilet tank. His white forehead arcs steeply up and back into his scalp. I was listening hard to his speech but can't hold on to its meaning. When he leads us out of the room, we look at each other: it's mindless and sick, the way we're surrendering to him. He could be bringing us to a firing squad.

In his bedroom, there's a TV and a VCR. He sits us down on the bed and floor. "I've taped some material," he says, punching buttons, "to ease the transition." The room fills with sitar twanging, and on the screen, his face as blank as the moon, is Buddha. Cross-legged, breasts hanging, the nest of his lap full of his eggy belly. The picture changes—water lilies on a pond. Then Buddha again. VV's face is lit by the screen. Though she's only in her thirties, maybe, her black hair, frizzed like a halo, is salted with white. There's no sickness showing. But up close, she's a plain person.

When I hear Cyril rewinding the tape I get mad at myself because I wasn't paying attention. I'm messing this up already. We go back to the living room. Geezer Leaflets is talking, looking around hungrily for listeners. "Live wrong," he says, "and you'll return as an insect."

"There we part company," says Softgoods. Divinity is looking serious. As we sit down in a circle, Pal farts, and VV stares—she thinks it was me.

2. We will be doing exercises to recover memories of past lives, if any. No phonies or thrill seekers.

When Pal and I arrived, VV and Cyril were the only ones here. She introduced us proudly as her students, as though she were donating us and wanted a receipt. Cyril's handshake has more expression than most people's whole faces. "Students! People who think!" His wide warm fingers, startlingly gentle for all that muscle, said we knew each other already. He'd rejected a lot of callers, he told us. Their words were perfect, but their intonations gave a different message. "If there's anything people don't understand," he said, "sooner or later, they'll destroy it." Cyril is hot, his shoulders and arms are about to explode. Even though his voice is soft, he sounds like it's hard for him not to shout.

A roaring rose outside, then stopped in front of the house. He smiled sadly and said, "An unfortunate example. Please wait." He went downstairs. Before he reached the bottom, the doorbell rang.

He was down there a long time. When I went to the

top of the stairs to look, Cyril was arguing with two bikers, *Zombies* swirled across their jackets. Chests were sticking out. He didn't want them to come up. Cyril moved close, talking low, and I was afraid they were going to hit him, but they backed away. His courage, his confidence, amazed me. "What're *you* looking at," one of them screamed at me—I laughed, I couldn't help it—before Cyril got them out the door and double-locked it.

When he came trotting back upstairs, he was calm. "Are they going to plague us?" VV asked. Like Cyril, she wasn't a bit afraid. "We can't have them. We'd never get anything done."

"They're good boys," he said. "But I told them the way it is."

3. Contribution per session: $2.

We gave him the money. Pal said, "Jesus, already?" and laughed.

"Artificial barrier," Cyril explained. "You can't make anything free."

I can see into the kitchen—pegboard walls, neatly hung with pans and household tools, their positions marked by black-painted silhouettes—where two coffee mugs stand on the table, and a woman's umbrella hangs from the back of a chair. On the counter, next to flour and sugar canisters, is an empty-looking terrarium. Cyril says there's a tarantula, hidden in its burrow. All these people make it shy. He has a tortoise, too, crawling around in a box of plywood and chicken wire. Before the meeting began, we all watched him feed it lettuce, which it ate with a slow, pawing motion of its head. When I remember what he said on the phone about reverence for life, I start to get worried, because I like squashing things, sometimes. Once, to see him do it, I bet Pal he wouldn't pour his goldfish down the garbage disposal. After that I bet he wouldn't put the cat in the microwave, and he wouldn't.

"The point is," Divinity is saying, "the soul goes to heaven or hell." Pal makes a sound as though he's loosening mucus. VV looks up. A disturbance in class! Her eyeglasses are huge. Their frame is the color of a lime Popsicle licked practically through, and the nosepiece curves as if she's got a third eye. I want to lift them off her face. One lens looks incredibly thick. It refracts a slice of wall, jigsawing a crescent out of her head.

She says to Divinity, "So there's nothing left to reincarnate, is there."

"On the other hand," Divinity says, "doesn't the immortality of the soul imply its pre-existence?" I know these points are key, but the instant I think about them I lose them. In our family, no one has been to church in years. God exists, I know. He's like the largest prime number. You can't deny that there has to be one, but thinking about it is no fun, and no help.

> 4. Tonight (Session 1): (A) Each student will explain his or her interest in the subject. (B) Desensitization to the death trauma.

VV is listening, sucking her lower lip. She snaps open her bag, pulls out a pen and an index card. As she writes, her chin is lowered. This position makes a crease ring her neck as though her head had been severed and glued back on. When I start picturing how that would be done, I make myself feel sick. "In essence, I'm a seeker," says Divinity, and he folds his hands.

Everyone looks around the circle. "I'm not prepared, teacher," says Softgoods.

5. No liquor or drugs. No sexual game playing.

6. Treat as sensitive material. Western society is hostile to reincarnation. Keepa da mouth shut.

Cyril says, "How about you."

He means Poncho. "I didn't write anything down," she says.

"Looks like no one else did either." He aims a cannon, his big white forehead, at each of us in turn.

"Well," she says, "this isn't really the same. Oh, maybe it is. I just think we're all the same person."

People like her take something out of me, I don't know what. They make me feel it's less impressive to be a human being. She says, "I had this vision once. Like our bodies? Plants grow out of us? And animals eat the plants? And we eat the animals?"

VV and I look at each other. Then we get up to leave. We drive to her place, where she pours drinks while I build a fire. "Now," she says, settling into the sofa, "we can continue the conversation in a more intelligent manner." *A few minutes later, arms around one another, they lay on the carpet before the fireplace.*

I'm sure I made an idiotic sound, but nobody's looking. "The only thing, as far as drugs," Poncho says, tapping

Cyril's handout with her fingernail, "some grass. Some weed would help a lot. Some locoweed."

Cyril pats the air—a delicate gesture for his thick hand and arm—tamping the idea back into its container. "Not now," he says. "I have my reasons." He turns to Pal. "How about you?"

And Pal's already nodding. I want to tell Cyril he's making a mistake. Pal leans forward, hands clasped. He says, "I don't know when or where this was, but I used to live in a jungle."

As a jungle boy, Pal was disadvantaged—born a dwarf. When both his parents were killed by cobras, he was too young to join the hunters, so he lived on roots and larvae. But the witch doctor told him about an ancient lost city, three days' walk from their village. A wild elephant carried him there, with a bodyguard of tigers. I know exactly what this is, a movie we saw when we were little. Pal looks at me innocently. He sweeps back his hair to show a scar—once, when his father was dragging him to his room, he deliberately smashed his head through a window. "I received this," he explains, "when the tower fell. I was reborn with the identical mark."

I've been sinking in my chair, and now I realize I'm exhausted. My father was right—this group's not legitimate. Either that or I'm the one who's not. I feel burglarized, full of space where something important used to be. When Cyril smiles at me next, smiles and nods, I don't care anymore. He smiles like that at everyone. Maybe all he wants from this are friends. I tug the sheets of paper from my back pocket, warm from being sat on, folded in quarters and curled to the curve of my hip.

"I see *somebody* did the assignment," he says.

And then, because it'll sound as stupid as everything else I've heard here, I can't read it. I DON'T KNOW WHO I AM. I DON'T KNOW WHAT I AM. I DON'T KNOW WHAT I'M PART OF. How can I read them that?

"I saw this in the paper," I say, unfolding my other sheet. "I thought it was pretty interesting. U.S. studying likelihood of reincarnation."

U.S. STUDYING
LIKELIHOOD OF
REINCARNATION

A top-secret government commission has been conducting an urgent study of reincarnation "in all its aspects," a high Defense Department official confirmed yesterday.

The official, who declined to be identified, was responding to rumors prevalent in government circles in recent weeks.

The study, said to have been ongoing for six months, is being conducted by a C.I.A.-led task force reporting to the National Security Council and the President.

Neither the C.I.A. nor the White House would respond to questions. It has been widely speculated that vital strategic issues may be at stake.

If reincarnation could be demonstrated, theories of first-strike survival might have to be modified. The concept of deterrence, which has been widely credited with averting nuclear war, could become outmoded.

"The Soviets are on to this too," commented a Senate aide, requesting anonymity. "We're all very tense. It's like the race for an A-bomb, or getting a man on the moon."

When I finish, everyone's talking at once. VV says she finds this frankly hard to credit. Pal just laughs at me, he knows me pretty well. But Cyril is nodding. "We'll watch our security," he says. I know I should tell him I made it up, but I don't want to. I still feel robbed. And no matter where the details came from, the idea is logical. "Let us bow our heads," he says.

"What about you?" says Poncho. "It's your turn."

"No," Cyril says, "we've done enough. Item B, we'll wait until next week. But let's share three minutes of silent communion."

The tortoise is crawling around in its box. Its claws scratch and slide, it bangs its shell against the wood. I keep my head down, but I can't close my eyes.

7. Finally, be sure you are in good health. We may be using trance states, etc, that will put a strain on your system. Have you ever had heart trouble? Epilepsy? Been treated for any nervous disorder?

Across the circle, VV's thin ankles drop from her pantslegs, her feet are lined up in low-heeled shoes.

"Okay," says Cyril. "Beautiful."

"No," I say, "it's not beautiful."

"No?"

I don't even know why I opened my mouth. But they're all watching me, and I swear it, VV is smiling. Cyril nods. "Come back strong."

"I don't know," I say. And I don't, except that nothing has happened. I'm outside, still in darkness, looking at VV's feet, the same way I look at parts of her in class.

She knows it. She rests one on top of the other. Her shoes are shabby, and I want to buff them up.

"It's slow," Cyril tells me sympathetically. "But stick with me and I'll make you an angel."

Pal warbles in a falsetto, flapping his elbows, and Cyril laughs. "A kind of angel," he says. "Call it whatever you want." By now everybody is standing. "Same time next week. *Arrivederci.*"

"God bless you all," says Geezer Leaflets. "Read those, okay? Two minutes out of your busy day."

At the door, Softgoods tells Pal and me, "I'm heading over to Sullivan's." Up close you can see he isn't even middle-aged, he's old. His face hangs as if he bought it secondhand. "Would you guys want to come for a drink, talk a little more?"

"Sullivan's?" Pal asks, and I don't know what's coming, but I turn away.

"I'm driving," Softgoods says, "if you—"

"Sullivan's, right," Pal says. "Isn't that a faggot bar?"

"Eat shit," says Softgoods, and he runs down the stairs.

The rain has stopped. The windshield is so clean it's invisible. But once we're on the Connecticut Turnpike, westbound headlights sprinkle the glass with sparks where it's chipped. I tell Pal, "That was pretty rude."

"Let him play with his own dork." He rolls down his window and sticks his head out and screams, "*Let him play with his own dork!*" Then he starts talking about all the assholes that were there tonight. V. Victor is hot for me, he says, he was watching her while I read my story. And he really likes the Bull, which is what he's calling Cyril. "You can tell," Pal says, "*he* never licked anyone's rosy red rectum." I just lean over the wheel, bumping my forehead against it to make sure I'm awake.

Finally I see Woody's flagpole. In the driveway, Pal gets out, still talking, then leans back in. "Did you lamp the pussy?"

"Yeah." I know he means Poncho.

"I'd like to stuff it down her throat. Beat off, is my advice." He slams the door. "Or you'll have a wet dream," he says against the window, and licks the glass, a curling stroke with the point of his tongue.

Farther up Deer Hill Road, I turn in at our mailbox. I barely inch the Volks along our crunching gravel drive. If I wake them, they'll yell from their bedroom, wanting to know how it went, whether I had fun. I let myself in the kitchen door. Climbing the stairs in the dark, I keep close to the wall, where the boards don't groan as much.

Outside their open door, I stop. I look in but can't see anything. All I hear is one slow rising and falling breath, like the house itself breathing. I wish I could stand in the dark and listen all night. But I go on down the hall to my room, because I'm starting to feel very funny. The way a space probe or something would feel, heading away from earth—not because it wants to, just because it was made that way, because its builders built it like that, to go and never come back.

FIVE

Drones can't sting, I'm always careful to explain. But by the time I do my final demonstration, children always forget. "What's going on?" I ask the class. "Seems to be something in my ear!" Eli, to show how unbearably I'm embarrassing him, rolls back his head as if I just chopped through his spine. I bend my earflap forward with a fat drone trapped inside, buzzing like a bandsaw. The kids are screaming, the teacher has both hands over her mouth. When I shout "Oop-la!" and out he flies, the teacher applauds—Harriet used-to-be-Lesnesky, girl from the South End—and the class obediently joins in.

There in the sun and the hum, the children's applause and the honey scent, I'm so happy I can't believe I'd ever change anything. This is my family right here. "Jerry," says Harriet, wincing when a bee comes near, "*thank* you. Third-graders, *thank* Mr. Hook."

Then they're heading for their yellow bus, parked beyond the honey house, and my pleasure is gone, my life feels finished. Ended by my own decision, even though nothing has actually happened. All Mangiacapra did, that silver fox, was nod at me. Nod and smile. Smile and nod. He wouldn't say what he'd pay, or even if he'd buy. I'd brought a surveyor's map of my property, and Mangiacapra put on horn-rimmed glasses to study it. That always makes me afraid I've stepped in over my depth—when the other person, who I didn't know wore them, puts on a pair of glasses.

Then he started to write down dimensions. Without a word. On his desk lay his alligator-grain briefcase, jaws open. I looked into it: a mistake. It had those built-in file dividers, full of deals and documents from a world I'll never know. On one wall, a religious calendar showed a haloed saint beside a laden ass. Thumbtacked below it, snapshots of Mangiacapra's daughters. He's naming his streets for them. Cecilia Drive, Annette Circle, Imogene Terrace, Barbara Place. "Lovely girls," I told him. But he only nodded and smiled, silent.

The third grade is back in its bus and I wave as they roll down my driveway, arms semaphoring behind dusty glass. Helen comes out of the house, saying "Back in a few hours." She has her sample bag, off to scout for new accounts. "Eli, try to help your father."

I say, "Good luck out there."

"Luck?"

It's humbling, all she can put into a single word—amusement, surprise, contempt. In the South End, we spoke whole speeches, as though we couldn't trust each other to understand. But nobody spoke against luck. We believed in luck. Helen angles her long body into the Beetle; she's in an excellent mood. "Work hard," she tells us, me and Eli, out the window: the same way that Marigolde would have said "Take it easy." Watching her pull away, I'm ready to walk into the kitchen and write *These have been wonderful years, you've taught me a lot,* and be gone.

"Let's get started." Eli's fallen into a daydream—what of? His pale face points blindly into the distance, his lips tremble as he whispers. Ten years ago I'd hug him, seeing that. "Wake up."

"Okay," he says. "I said I'd help. Should I pretend this is how I really want to spend the day?"

"Yes. Try pretending." I'm getting angry in a way that has no pleasure in it. "Look at yourself. It's going to be warm."

But he's indifferent to weather. Today he's wearing a suede vest over his wool shirt. Eli is indifferent, unconscious, to practically everything. It's not a phase he's in, nothing to do with reincarnation, this so-called group. It's who he always was. A baby who never cried because nothing bothered him. You'd kiss and nuzzle him everywhere without his noticing. "If the leather gets you stung," I tell him, "blame yourself."

"*Que será, será,*" he says. As we walk out to the truck, he unbuttons the vest and shrugs it off.

We don't extract and bottle till fall. Our little bit of spring honey—apple blossom and some clover—we package right in the comb, under clear plastic: pretty item, and higher profit. Today we're giving the bees the four-by-four frames to fill. These are in fresh hive boxes, cleaned during winter and freshly painted, piled now on the truck bed.

Because I expect to find trouble, we start with the

hives that Eli's in charge of. The first isn't bad. I scrape off the queen cells and don't tell him he's been lazy. "Dreaming again?" He's standing in the fly line, asking to be stung. Then he'll be as furious as though I'd slapped him. I go on to the next hive. Eli wakes up enough to say, "There's no queen in there. Want me to go back and get one?"

But I stop and look at the hive. "They're happy," I tell him. The sound is good, the traffic so thick the returning bees are stacked up waiting to land. "You sure?"

He only sighs, to say I'm wasting my time. We light the smoker and tranquilize the brood chamber. I lift out the center frame. "If there's no queen, what laid these grubs?" Then, tilting the frame so sunlight fills the bottoms of the cells, I can even show him eggs.

With Eli, nothing is ever enough. "Then where is she?" As if he might still be right. And then of course I can't find her. I pull out another frame—more eggs, more grubs—there has to be a gorgeous queen, hidden among the workers.

Now I'm angry again and Eli has his small smile. "Well, she's here," I say. "I can't spend all day finding her for you. You'd have noticed the grubs and eggs," I tell his smart face, "if you'd looked for them." My anger doesn't hurt anymore because I'm losing control and it feels perfect, a surrender as easy as sledding downhill. "This damned group is on your mind too much. You ought to taper it off."

He does something with his shoulders that he used to do when he was little. I see how slippery love is—release its neck for one minute, set it down like your keys or reading glasses, and it's gone. I remember diapering this man, bathing him in the kitchen sink. "Wean yourself away," I tell him. "You're not a baby anymore."

"I don't expect you to understand," he says. "To you, I'm a stranger."

Though this is what I've been thinking too, I tell him not to be silly.

"I am, Dad. This isn't my home."

"No?"

"You don't have to sound like that. I'm not saying you mistreated me."

"You'd better not."

"You and Mom aren't my right parents, that's all." He sees how mad I'm getting and says, "Don't worry. It isn't anyone's fault."

"And who the hell," I ask, "do you think you are?"

This makes him laugh. Then he says, "Hey. Dad?"

I know from his face that I'm falling. Black comes in from the edges. The orchard tilts. I go down, catching the earth with one knee and both hands. In another second, light and sound return, I'm on my feet and dusting off my pants. Eli looks scared and holds my shoulders, and no matter what he says, I'm his right father.

By midday we have to go home and get more hive boxes. They're in the storeroom of the honey shed, behind the extractor. I haul them out and hand them up to him, standing straddle-legged on the bed of the truck. Arranging items of any sort is the kind of job you can give Eli. While he's tugging and tapping his stacks straight, I go up to the house and make us sandwiches. We eat, sucking Coke from foaming cans, as we drive back through the orchard.

I'm thinking again about his group. He's gone three times, and all I know is what I knew at the start: "Cyril" and a phone number. It was in the Personals column, he said, but Eli doesn't read the paper, not even the headlines. Not the sports, not the comics, certainly not the classifieds. "Let me guess," I say when we're working again, "who told you about this so-called group." He doesn't answer. We're over a hive, leaning into the vortex of bees. "This so-called teacher?"

"Cut it out."

Usually I would, but when we're wearing our veils I feel different. "Be careful of older women," I tell him. "They're desperate, a lot of them."

"Damn it!" he screams.

It takes me a minute to figure out he's been stung. He's throwing himself all over and won't let me scrape off the stinger. "Are you still using that spray-can stuff? They can't stand the smell of you. Hold still or they'll get you again."

Then he's perfectly calm. "Yes," he says. "It's that basic, isn't it."

"What?"

"Basic chemistry."

I tell him that's a weakling's excuse, though I'm not sure I know what he means.

"Listen," he says. "I'm through." And he takes off his veil and gloves and lays them on the grass.

I watch him walk away toward home. Shouting won't do any good—from how he's leaning, the swing of his arms, he's gone beyond recalling. I try to pretend that he's not just quitting work. He's leaving home. I'll worry, but this will liberate us both. The daydream's good for half an hour. Then, after I'm done with the section and back in the truck on my way to Marigolde's, I give it up. He'll be in his room when I get home, his door closed. Later he'll come downstairs and arrange the dinner plates and knives and forks as if his life depended on it.

At Marigolde's, there's a pickup in the driveway.

BOWLERS HAVE BIGGER BALLS

Caution: This Vehicle Stops
for Chicks, Foxes, Beavers, and Pussies

IF YOU CAN READ THIS *beware of farts*

It's Ken. When I walk in he'll leave, if he has any decency. And Ken has. South End decency. He can't stay off her—the whole time she and I were married, he used to come by for beers. But poor people know about rank. Crowded families know about waiting in line.

Her rain gutters look good for another winter, but her window trim needs paint. When the door opens, they're standing side by side, Marigolde in her dental receptionist's uniform. No matter how many years she's worked, her official whiteness makes me nervous. "Jerry," she says, sounding glad I'm here.

"You going out? Hi, Ken."

"Just back."

"Hookie." Ken is perspiring—why is he perspiring?—and holding a can of beer. He raises it and drinks. His eyes close. The arrogance of handsomeness: his neck is unshaven, creases filled with dirt. He spreads both hands on his belly and gives a long, complicated belch—you can see his pride at getting off a good one, then his delight as it goes on and on. He talks football awhile. He talks movies. He imitates Brando portraying a Mexican. Ken is a filthy puppy, a man you probably love if you can stand him at all. Finally he leaves, swinging his truck onto the lawn to get around mine behind him. Where he was parked, fluid gleams on the driveway.

"God," she says. She acts it out, *relief*, the way the Smalls always do, drawing the back of one hand and then the other across her forehead, flapping them in the air to get rid of the sweat. "He was here waiting when I got home."

In the living room I kiss her. But after a minute, two minutes, I need to be in the open air. "Talk while I work?" Marigolde just looks at me. She wants us to go upstairs. She grabs both my ears and pinches hard enough to hurt.

I bring the truck around, and when she meets me in back she's changed into jeans. We unstack Eli's towers and carry the boxes down the terraced lawn. While she feeds the smoker, I tell her how he walked away. Now, though I'm trying not to—he's old enough to be his own problem!—I'm giving in to worry. "I think he's deteriorating. This group has affected his mind. What should I do? Should I go to the college?"

"Talk to someone. That's right." She squeezes the

bellows, stirs the burning twigs, squeezes again. "It shouldn't be all on you."

"In here."

She pumps. I lift the lid and add a box, trying not to crush any bees. An inch from my left eye, a worker buzzes at my veil, rear legs gold-ringed with pollen. I straighten, easing my back.

"Dodo." She presses her veil against mine. "You dumb donkey." Through the mesh, her teeth shine. "What about the other parents with kids in this group?"

"I'm not that kind of hero." I imagine myself leading a band of fathers and mothers, pushing in to break up a meeting. And though it's only an idea, I feel my body getting ready to fight. I'm rolling on the ground with the famous Cyril, who in this scene is fat and bald and shouts, as a war cry, his telephone number.

When I get home, Helen has returned. She's on her knees in the garden, long arms brown at the elbow. I drop to a squat and ask her, "How'd it go?"

"What are you smiling about? What happened here while I was gone?" Raising a three-clawed cultivator, she wipes her forehead with her wrist. Her eyeglass lenses show the paths of drops of sweat.

"Nothing happened, an argument. Is he upstairs?"

"He's gone, I couldn't stop him. He'll telephone. That was all he said."

It seems impossible. I feel afraid, as though I've just found someone else's wallet and may not give it back. "Was he mad?"

"No. Mad? I don't know. Yes, of course he was mad."

"Crying?"

"I said wait, let's talk about it. He went up and packed some clothes and books. I watched him. Crying? Only me."

I picture her there in his room, sitting on the bed while he prepares to go, and I take her muddy hand to help her up from her knees. Maybe it's my fault he left, because I'm greedy, call it cruel. Pretty soon I'll hurt her worse than he did. But as I tug her to her feet, a new weight, palm to palm, frightens me. I never wanted her to feel this. For her, I'll have to get him home.

We go inside and sit at the kitchen table with glasses of ice water. "You'll have to see this teacher," she says, "and don't look like that. It's not even four. She might still be in her office. Just say you're concerned about him. Go now. Tomorrow it will be all over town."

This is so much like Helen, the Underwoods, the North End—worrying over gossip, not her son—that I make a gesture. Not at her, I wouldn't do that. But she flinches, flinging her face to the side, dodging the possible slap. And then I realize how intensely I've been wanting to hit Eli, Ken, Cyril, really anyone.

"Sorry," I say. "I'll go, I'll see her. I'll explain that we're concerned about him."

As soon as I'm in the Beetle, though, I get out and slam the door. What can I say to this woman professor? The fact is that I need him out of my way. I feel as filthy as Ken—what I want right now is a bath. It's the clearest feeling I've had all day. I want to be clean and sweet-smelling and by myself, to lock the bathroom door and get into the tub with some magazines and soak and read.

I lean against the car with my eyes closed. For maybe three minutes it feels okay not to be doing a single thing. All this time, Helen is watching me from the kitchen window. I don't have to look.

I drive down Barnum Avenue into Bridgeport, past locations where I still imagine the barbers and tobacconists and soda shops of our childhood. Now it's all chiliburgers and tacos. Japanese and German car dealerships. Finally I pass the cemetery, about the only place that hasn't changed. When I was Eli's age, I liked to walk through and read the stones—people of every age and nationality—and try to form an opinion of their lives.

The college parking lot is bigger than I remembered, and the building itself, a converted munitions factory, looks like a fortress. There are still guys living whose hands got blown off, working there. You'll see one, sometimes, coming out of a tavern, or in the produce aisle, shopping with his daughter, guiding the cart with his hook. I climb the steps, feeling light-headed. Inside the double doors, next to an overflowing garbage pail, is an old man. The garbage pail is full of dolls, parts of dolls—dolls ripped and smashed into bits. He smiles and I'm frightened he wants to shake, but he's only offering me a pamphlet. As he flips it open I see a tiny arm, perfect to the fingertips, reaching out from a pool of blood in a white basin.

The main corridor is so empty I walk on my soles, turning to look behind me. Somewhere a computer printer is chattering and beeping. I spot a directory with the woman's name, **V Victor, Dept of Phys Sci.** Her office is easy to find, an innocent door in a row of doors, and I'm there, knocking, with no idea what I'll say, hoping a father will have an instinct.

"Come in?"

Virginia Victor is a small woman, maybe forty, behind a messy desk. When our eyes meet, it hits me that she doesn't, couldn't possibly, know who I am. It's an advantage I can't give up, the only thing that gives me power against her. "I'm a student," I say. "An older student." I'll get the feel of her before I tell my name.

"A mature student." She's got me placed. "I'm afraid I only have a minute."

"Sure. Not right now, but I thought next fall I'd take some courses, so I've been knocking on doors. Can I ask what you teach?"

"Biological science." She smiles. "Not everyone's cup of tea. Don't you have a catalogue?" She hands me one. "You may keep this."

"I'm interested, though."

"Are you? What's your job?"

"Retired." Eli might have told her that his father keeps bees. "I worked at Stratford Plating twenty-three years. Took early retirement because of my heart."

"And your name?"

"Seth. Seth Mangiacapra."

"Well, Seth, mature students often do enjoy my courses. People your age, even my age, have learned to value knowledge. To me the most important thing is understanding the world around me. At least trying to understand. If we don't even try, do we deserve to live at all?"

Is she crazy, would she sleep with a student? "And what do you think of reincarnation?" I'd like to ask her.

How can I go back to Helen and say she's nice? She's nice. But I don't like her, don't like liking her—she's already started to seduce me.

"And what," she says, "are *your* interests?"

I back up against the door. When I kick it with my heel I think for a second that I've set off an alarm—a beating bell so loud I cover my ears. She laughs. "I have a committee. I hope to see you here next term, Seth."

And what about my son? She's standing, briefcase swinging in her hand, coming toward me. Now I don't know why I lied. Was that a father's instinct? I didn't even ask her help—another instinct? Wasn't in, couldn't find her, is all I can tell Helen now. Out in the corridor, which has narrowed to a tiled tunnel, doors are swinging open. In a few seconds the space is packed with college students. The squeeze of them weakens me, so many young people together. It's all their hair, their bare skin. The smell of their bodies is like a sandwich with mayonnaise left in the sun. They press tighter, harder, until I'm pinned to the wall. The corridor is suddenly hot and I turn, fighting my way outside.

In the parking lot I'm panting, amazed at myself and ashamed. These aren't feelings I know—it's how Eli must feel in a crowd. Does he get that from me, or can it work the other way? Next to my car, revving an enormous bike, is a man the size of a child. This can't possibly be safe: his toes stretch to touch the pedals. His engine starts popping and dies. I hear a sound like someone swatting a fly and a thick gob of spit hits the asphalt. He gazes somewhere near my eyes, as if I might be there or not.

Heading home, I keep remembering how fine I felt

this morning, talking to Harriet's third-graders. And I try to figure out when, exactly what moment, things began to go wrong. My sense of time is twisting, though, the way time must in a beehive, in the dark where birth and death go on forever. When I wonder if anything ever began, or ever ended, I feel like Eli again.

On Deer Hill Road I drive slowly, looking into the apple trees. My veil and gloves are home. But I turn off the pavement onto the trail through the orchards. Where the ruts get too deep, I stop the car and walk. I come up behind Eli's hive, the supposedly queenless one, and gradually raise the cover. The hum envelops me as the bees swirl out, bump me and bounce, land and crawl on my face. I place my fingers one at a time and lift the center frame. There she is. I hold her by the wings—the long-bodied, egg-full queen—and when I put her down, she's left me her scent. Her daughters, like babies of mine, hug my fingertips.

FROM OLD TO NEW

Balling the Queen

Very often when the bees decide they will not accept the queen let loose among them they will begin to pull at her, piling on her in such numbers that they form a ball around her. Every bee in the ball will seem intent on pulling her limb from limb. Unless the owner comes to her rescue she may be stung to death or be suffocated.

When queens were introduced in the old-fashioned way—that is, before cages were constructed so as to release queens automatically—much trouble was encountered by bees balling queens. If they were not ready to accept her when she was released by the apiarist, they were pretty sure to ball her. Right here is a point that it is well to observe: When the bees let out the queen they very rarely ball her. But when it is necessary for the apiarist *to perform the work of opening the hive and making a general disturbance, there is danger of balling. Suppose she is balled. The ball should be lifted out of the hive and smoke blown on it until the bees come off one by one, but hot smoke must not be blown on the queen. When the queen is found, get hold of her wings and pull the rest of the bees off her by their wings. Cage her again as at first, and give her another trial. The advice has been given to drop the queen, when she is balled, into a vessel of luke-warm water. The angry bees will immediately desert the queen, [at which point] she can easily be taken out of the water and recaged.*

Another way of saving the queen without having to recage her is to carry a small oil can with a spring bottom, such as is used on a sewing machine, filled with thin syrup. When the bees are found balling her, saturate the ball thoroughly by pressing hard on the bottom of the can, causing the syrup to penetrate the ball. Close the hive and the bees will turn their attention to cleaning themselves and the queen. . . . She will be accepted without further trouble.

—ABC and XYZ of Bee Culture

SIX

UNIVERSALITY OF REINCARNATION ASSUMED BY PLATO, BUDDHA—YET NON-BELIEVERS EQUALLY FIRM—WHY?

Extortion, Pal said admiringly. The Bull was bleeding Eli, charging him a fucking fortune for one shitty room. But Eli felt that he was in the right place. He could smell Long Island Sound, and waking in the night he could hear it. His parents' confusion had been painful—when he'd returned for more clothes, they hadn't known whether to threaten or beg—and he had seen that explaining would make it worse. Why explain, when they must feel it too: how all three of them had been dishonest. His answer to shouting was silence.

By September, it had become clear that he wasn't going back to college. His first job had been in a warehouse, a catacomb of aisles buzzing with fluorescent light that plinked him like a banjo string. Now he worked for a caterer. That was better, even flinging food onto plates, even scraping it off with his fingers into a garbage pail.

After they'd aligned the tables in some church basement or social hall, he laid out settings in eighty-foot rows; and there would be a moment—before the guests all pushed in, babbling, wrenching back chairs, kneeing tables so that iced tea slopped from pitchers and flatware jangled—when he could stand alone, hands clasped behind his back, and survey the ordered room. The pay was bad, but Cyril believed it was healthier for him to be working.

At meetings now, he never knew who would appear. Once a dark-bearded man in a turban; young girls, sometimes, splitting with giggles. Lately Mondo, with his dancer's body and eyes of an animal waking up. As the week and day shrank to the hour, Eli waited for VV—she came sometimes, sometimes not. Pal came for meetings and came other nights, too. He and Cyril would go out together, looking for women. They'd bring them back to Cyril's apartment, where Eli lay in bed, listening.

UNIVERSALITY OF REINCARNATION ASSUMED BY PLATO, BUDDHA—YET NON-BELIEVERS EQUALLY FIRM—WHY?

ANSWER: *BOTH* MAY BE RIGHT.

Concerning Cyril himself, Eli was still trying to think, trying to understand the man. He'd once been a biker, a Zombie in fact—that much Eli could believe. But he also claimed that he'd founded the club, that he used to lead them everywhere, on rides past Niagara Falls into Canada, rides to Florida, once to Mexico, dozens of big bikes, gone for weeks, camping by roadsides, blasting down the highway two by two. As he described those days, Cyril's eyes would water so that he had to blink and wipe them, laughing at himself. What percent of that could be true? Now the Zombies were jealous that he'd evolved. They wanted him back to lead them again. This man in his forties, who sometimes talked like an encyclopedia?

But it couldn't have been them, he said—they respected him too much—when his apartment was broken into a few weeks after Eli moved there. During the night, someone entered through a window. Eli woke at dawn with strong hands shaking him: Cyril was terrified. In the living room, bulging red hieroglyphics had been sprayed on the walls, a boast or warning that they couldn't decipher. A sharp chemical smell hung in the air, and a hole had been burned in the center of the carpet.

The microwave was gone from the kitchen countertop. They'd come into Cyril's bedroom and taken his watch from his bedside table, his wallet from his trousers. The VCR had been amputated, leaving stumps of severed cables and a dust-free rectangle where it had stood. Eli's bedroom looked unentered—why hadn't they stolen his wallet too? Grateful, he nevertheless felt himself denied, set apart. Back in the living room, Cyril stared at an open desk drawer that had held albums of stamps. A collection he'd been adding to since childhood. Then he swore and slumped down on the sofa. He was still naked, which was how he slept, and looked so vulnerable that Eli came and sat next to him in his pajamas. "Do you work today?" Cyril asked. "Can you stay home?"

"Sure," said Eli. "It's okay." Cyril drew up his knees and hugged them. It was the posture of someone doomed, the position that American Indians were supposed to be buried in. Eli tried to beam calming landscapes, soothing colors, into Cyril's mind, and soon Cyril gained enough strength to dress and cook them some pancakes. His arm around Eli's shoulders, he said he was glad *someone* understood his nature, interpreted him correctly, because almost nobody else in the world ever did or would or could. This speech, Eli felt, was to keep him from leaving, but he didn't want to leave.

The tarantula was safe at the bottom of its burrow. They found the tortoise out on the sidewalk, dead in its cracked shell. Cyril wrapped it in newspaper and placed it gently in the garbage pail, while Eli thought of bloody ways they could have been murdered in their beds. Adopting the poor tortoise, Cyril said, had been his mistake. They lived too long to be pets; they became like people—just as parrots did. Back upstairs, he showed Eli an empty birdcage. A neighbor lady had given him a blue and green beauty, making him swear he'd never give it to the zoo. But years later, when he'd returned it to her (his new girl friend was hyperallergic to birds), the old bitch had given it to the zoo herself! There the parrot had soon grown bald, continually reaching up (he twisted, demonstrating) to claw its head, and would no longer speak. Cyril believed that it had gone insane.

This story left Cyril sad again. They drove to the pet store, where he chose a pair of green snakes with pale bellies and busy, intelligent tongues. That night, as the snakes flowed around and around their new tank on the kitchen counter, Cyril and Eli stayed up late. Vivaldi on the stereo, they purified their walls, laying on swaths of white with dripping rollers.

The next day Cyril installed motion detectors wired to a siren alarm. He secured the downstairs door with a brass chain. But he told the group that violence must be met with peace, and he gave them silk ribbons for spirituality, white for males, red for females, to be worn next to the skin. Such superstition surprised Eli, who hid his ribbon in his underwear drawer.

Cyril too came from Stratford, the South End. He was self-educated: self-invented, he said. He'd known, it turned out, Eli's father. Jerry Hook, one of the big kids then, wouldn't remember him, but he, Cyril, remembered perfectly Jerry and Jerry's girl friend, talking late under the street light, the girl they'd called, in junior high, Titanic Tits. Mary Small—not Mary, Marilyn. Marigolde, Eli said. Then he told Cyril that his father was still screwing her. Though that was something he wouldn't want anybody in the world to know, now he heard it come out of his mouth as a kind of gift. Cyril asked where and when, how often, for how long—all questions that Eli couldn't answer—and finally shook his head and laughed, saying good for Jerry: he'd invented himself too.

Cyril drove a cab. He met, he said, all types. He rescued collapsed drunks and brought them to the city shelter, though when one fucker threw up in his cab he'd dropped him (Eli winced, knowing it was false, ashamed of Cyril's bravado) into a canal. Once Cyril had brought home a run-over collie and kept it alive for a week with just the touch of his hands. The night it died, he got drunk and spoke like a poet about life and death. Then, driving home from the bar (Eli shouting and whispering to stop), tires shrilling, Cyril aimed his T-bird at every dog and cat they saw on the lamplit streets. No: pretended to aim. Later he pointed out reasonably that he hadn't hit anything. Nor had he meant to. The game had eased his grief.

He was tormenting. Bounding up in the morning, naked and full of song, he would dance around Eli, sparring with open hands, until Eli ran to his room and tilted a chair under the doorknob. He was generous. "Use everything," Cyril had said from the start, demonstrating the many buttons of the Cuisinart, the Betamax soon to be stolen, showing where spare keys for the house and the car were hidden. When he showered, he trustingly left rubber-banded rolls of bills in plain view on his bedroom dresser. He encouraged Eli to read: Cyril had two bright shelves of free trial selections from book clubs. They discussed for hours what Eli should do with his life. His opportunities were infinite, Cyril would insist, slicing celery for a salad, or toweling off his bulging chest.

Eli couldn't have lived with a slob, and Cyril was neat, he was more than neat. When anyone left a room, the light had to be shut off. The bathroom was to be kept clean, especially of hair. Any tool or pot or pan from the kitchen pegboard went back in its marked spot, exactly over its black-painted silhouette. Cyril showered several times a day. After urinating, he would wash his hands and also his dick.

"That's a rarity," Cyril said when Eli admitted that he was a virgin. Holding it in this long was an achievement. Eli could see, behind his enthusiasm, his shock. One day when he came home to the apartment, Cyril wasn't there, only a blonde girl in denim and leather. Her name was Stormy, and she explained that she was doing Cyril a favor. "No," said Eli, "that's okay." When he came in later, Cyril must have already received her report. Neither of them made any comment. Eli, who was grateful for the gesture, was afraid Cyril would feel insulted. His big face showed only perplexity and concern.

Between Cyril and VV, there was something, he'd seen it immediately—a meaning in their voices and postures. What was it? Cyril spoke of her kindly. When Eli asked if she had cancer, saying that was the rumor at school, he denied it with horror. He called her a lonely woman, one badly in need of love. But when Eli mentioned that she was intelligent, he laughed and agreed that she certainly was, from the neck up. *Que será, será.* Though in Eli's own opinion he was far handsomer—full head of hair, much better skin, bigger eyes with no red veins—when it came to women nobody matched Cyril. From out of nowhere, with no detectable prior arrangement (but Cyril never seemed surprised), they'd arrive to sleep with him.

Marie, a gaunt nurse, came in uniform past midnight, smelling of the hospital. She'd take Eli aside and quiz him fiercely about who else had been there. Sometimes Cyril telephoned her in a disguised voice. "*I am going to kill-l-l you,*" he would whisper hoarsely, winking at Eli, mimicking Eli's frown, until Eli went into his room and shut the door, swearing to himself that he'd never let Cyril do this to VV.

The darkness was absolute. Half in passion, half in fear, VV and Eli lay together. People were speaking near them. Reincarnation study groups, the Director said, his voice grating. The President sounded resigned; a painful duty lay before him: How bad is it? We're monitoring several, said the Director. The central cell is in Bridgeport. VV's arms tightened around him. Eli took her nipple in his mouth.

"Must have fainted. He was lying right on top of the hive," Uncle Woody said. "They'd stung him to death. Hardly knew it was him, he was so puffy."

Although he hoped they wouldn't die in his absence, Eli needed to see their deaths often. His father lay, besmeared, among the honey-oozing frames. He heard his mother scream in the overturned Volks, he saw her collapse in the kitchen, smashing her head on the stove. The house was silent then. At the end of afternoon, sunlight would slant across the faded rugs, touch the black-mouthed fireplace, finally brighten the banister, gliding upstairs on its stiff ascending dowels.

Once Pal told the group that a Stratford cop had questioned him about Eli. Pinhead Sherman, Eli guessed, a cousin to the Hooks. He hadn't told them he was related to a police officer. Cyril nodded as though he'd expected this. "We'll tighten our perimeter," he said. "So watcha you mouth. And when you come in, *knock*, yell who you are. We don't want Eli kidnaped."

Not now. Not when he felt as vulnerable as something tidal, half evolved. There was a picture in his head: himself on a sand bar, digging shellfish. The breakers toppling far from shore showed that this wasn't Long Island Sound. At first he'd been afraid it was a scene from some movie, or else a description he'd read in a book and forgotten. But a book wouldn't leave you with seabirds' calls, the curl of the note. Even a movie couldn't dilate your nostrils with the stink of seaweed, tide-sculpted into ropes and mounds, exhaling flies.

"Okay," Cyril said. "Who's not finished reading?"

UNIVERSALITY OF REINCARNATION ASSUMED BY PLATO, BUDDHA—YET NON-BELIEVERS EQUALLY FIRM—WHY?

ANSWER: *BOTH* MAY BE RIGHT.

IF ALL ARE REINCARNATED—WHY DO WE KNOW IT AND NOT THEM?

"What you're getting at here," said the Holy Father. Pal had begun calling the divinity student that, and the man had blushed but not objected. "What you're getting at here," the Holy Father said, "destroys the entire point. The upward trend needs to be universal."

"It's frightening," Cyril said gently. "We represent"—he went to the blackboard—"maybe this much of the population."

5%

"At *most*," he said, underlining powerfully, so that his chalk shrieked. "You can't blame them. They're just frozen at an earlier stage."

And Eli understood. "They're grubs."

Everyone looked at him.

"Grubs," said Cyril. "Hey, good."

VV said, "That's a very keen insight. The larva model is fine for now, let's keep it. Still, I think there's something even more basic here."

"Grubs, man," Pal said. He'd been saying "man" ever since Mondo started coming. "Squash the suckers."

Cyril was standing with hands on hips, looking around until he had everyone's attention. "If they're grubs, there are certain implications. First," he said, as the Holy Father began frowning and shaking his head, "you can forget about raising their consciousness."

"Cannibals, man," said Mondo. "They eat the missionaries."

"That's *right.*" Cyril often seemed pierced by a joke, as though it held more meaning than the speaker knew. "The C.I.A.'s already moving, as Eli reported. They don't even have to kill us—just destroy our cerebral cortex."

"A bit much," VV said, smiling, trying to kid him out of it. "A bit far."

And to Eli's relief—where did the guy get all this?—Cyril smiled too. Then he said, "Desensitization," and turned down the lights. This was the last chance, Eli felt, to admit he'd invented that newspaper article, about the government's reincarnation task force. But he could hear the Director's harsh whisper—*Our country's darkest hour*—and the President, who usually spoke so softly, whose answer now was a thunderclap—*It must be her finest hour*—and wouldn't give those voices away.

"Old age."

Eli leaned back, trying to feel his joints stiffen, blood run slow. Across the room, VV sighed and slumped, slacks riding up tight. "Sounds are growing softer," Cyril said. "Everything's fading. Getting dark. Hold your breath a little." VV's chest rose. Her cheeks puffed out. Eli closed his eyes. He no longer needed this exercise, but it would be snooty to say so.

"Fading, fading. Very sleepy. Very peaceful. Fa-a-ading." Cyril was whispering. "You think you're asleep." For a minute he was silent. Then he gave a sharp puff, like someone blowing out a candle.

Snakebite. Electric chair. The last death was torture by whoever loved you best. Eli didn't know which of his parents that was, but it was his father he could imagine doing it: after Eli turned on a light and there his father was with Marigolde, blinded eyes darting, white bodies curled like things you find under a rock. Once, back at the beginning, VV had lectured to the group about insubstantiality. Our matter consists only of atoms, our atoms merely of electrical charges. In his father, Eli felt that energy whirl. Reverse the charge of one electron and his whole personality could reformulate. He would wear a black mask, attack in silence with his hive tool, rip Eli's body apart with a glint of splintered bone, flung-aside organs pumping. Shivering, Eli felt daylight stroke him where he had been darkest.

The library exercise, which came next, was progressive. The first week they'd visualized only a flight of stone steps. The second week they'd seen themselves climb those steps to a great carved door. The third week they'd opened the door and seen the books, shelved in stacks, receding from the eye in innumerable rows, squat beneath a vaulted ceiling.

This library, Cyril had explained, held all the information in the world. That week he had stopped them at the door. But the following week he brought them as far as the card catalogue, where each of them looked up his own name. The week after that, they each found the right stack and the right shelf, walked along the shelf to the book with the right name gold-stamped on its spine. Cyril had let them hold, but not open, their books, blow off the satiny dust, smell the paper and glue.

Tonight he asked if they were ready for some reading. Then he closed his eyes. "Deep. Slow. Deep. Good. Re. Lax. Good. Deep." He swayed to the beat. He was already gone.

The granite steps, scalloped with age, were awkwardly low, so that Eli never knew whether to climb them two or one at a time. Inside—though all the chandeliers were burning, the place seemed empty—his footbeats echoed. He remembered exactly where it was.

ELI HOOK

He banged the book onto a table. It was exactly as Cyril had said: the last chapter was the life he remembered. And there were earlier chapters.

But the beginning was in a language like Latin or Greek. And the next section was equally frustrating—black Gothic type, some unreadable early form of English. As he turned pages, first singly, then in wads, he discovered shining illustrations. Photographs of a curving beach, and close-ups of a boy playing in the sand. The boy didn't resemble him. Nevertheless he recognized himself, better than in his parents' bedside snapshot of someone small in a birthday hat, cone-shaped like a wizard's.

When he opened his eyes, VV gave him a tired smile, as though he and she had shared some arduous success. She looked the most natural he'd ever seen her. And yet it wasn't natural. It was how movie actors looked, satisfied and intimate and limp, after the people they were pretending to be had made love. Cyril's eyes were closed. The Holy Father was retying his shoelaces. Pal seemed asleep. Mondo caught Eli's glance and held something up, between thumb and forefinger, inquiringly. "Adjourned," Cyril said, his eyes still shut. And in what might have been a blessing, he polished the air slowly with both his palms.

Eat whale, expand the cosmos, come with them, they told Eli, spend the night in Mondo's panel truck, wait for the sunrise over the water. When he wouldn't, Pal called him a pussy. But Mondo, as always, smiled. "You call it," he said. With some difficulty—the capsule stuck to his fingers—he dropped a little blue whale into Eli's shirt pocket.

Eli was almost asleep. But something was happening. VV, the last to leave, looked at her watch. There was a problem, battery problem, car problem. "Why not stay," Cyril suggested.

But no, VV couldn't, her dog needed to be let out. And then Cyril tossed a jingling ring of keys, which Eli snatched from the air. He felt stunned, unprepared, as though caught by death or some great honor.

Outside, it had grown chilly. Moisture had condensed on the dented Thunderbird; by morning there would be frost. Eli found the wipers. The neon sign of Armando's Pizza Bar irradiated the misted rear window with pulsing light.

They rolled through empty streets, past factories and warehouses, under the Connecticut Turnpike. This, Eli knew, was it—what he'd thought about during every class, and still imagined in bed each night. Its suddenness made him drive slowly. He was afraid of failing her. Inexperience wouldn't matter if life worked as he believed, if you moved toward truth blindly, the way rivers feel for the sea. Yet Pal had explained, with a kind of dreamy delight, that it was physiologically possible to commit a grotesque and offensive blunder. Downtown looked abandoned, evacuated in preparation for war. A traffic light held them absurdly at a deserted intersection, and Eli could hear the clicking of its control box. Glancing at her, he touched his crotch: nothing. That worried him. As he accelerated, a roar arose behind them, and two Zombies, blond hair floating, staring straight as ships' figureheads, pulled alongside and slowly past. One might have been a girl—Stormy?

VV lived in a complex of garden apartments. "Come in," she told him. Stacks of books lay on the carpet, open magazines, folded newspapers. On the dinette table were rubber-banded piles of notecards, a set chessboard (were they going to play?), and the stiffening remains of a meal. There was a piercing smell. "Sally? I think she did let go." Reaching behind a sofa, VV hauled out a fat, short-legged thing by the collar. "It's not her fault." She put the dog outside, but it stayed against the door, scratching and whining, until she allowed it back in. It wedged itself behind the sofa again.

"Sit." She pointed to the sofa. Eli, though he didn't want to touch anything, even through his clothes, sat. "Do you drink red wine?" She put on a record—an opera. The orchestra churned to dizzying peaks. The room filled with inhuman trembling voices.

They drank. She lay with her head in his lap. He wanted to ask her so much—who she was, whether he'd known her in another life, what was going to happen to them now. At a crescendo, the music suddenly stopped, was followed by metallic clicks, plastic taps, and began again. She told him she'd been married at nineteen, but then, though he watched her mouth, he let her voice fall away as she talked and talked about her husband and their divorce. When she spilled wine on her blouse he mopped it up with his sleeve. She began to cry. He stroked her head, unprepared for the prominences of skull beneath the stiff hair. At a moment he felt he hadn't chosen, obeying the certainty that he was going to, he bent his head and kissed her. He felt as free of will as a stone skipped sidearm over water, settling into the dark at last.

She grabbed his head, crushing their lips and teeth together. Her wet mouth tasted of wine. Her tongue was powerful and grainy. Eli could still breathe through his nose. When the music stopped, he heard the dog wheezing behind the sofa. More clicks, a tap, and the trembly voices returned.

As they undressed she said, "I hope this doesn't bother you."

"What?"

"This." She was lying on her back. "My tits."

She sat up, and when they hung he saw what she

meant. It looked as if somebody had squeezed the left one so hard that it had emptied, swelling the right. Breast cancer? There wasn't any scar. Her upper arms, her belly, were slack, her thighs rippled like a sand bar. Trying to remember how he'd imagined her body, Eli realized that he never had.

"Have you ever done this before?" she asked, but he knew she knew the answer. "It's the most natural thing in the world. Come here." She stroked his face. "You're very attractive. I'd love to teach you." After another minute she said, sounding puzzled, "You don't have to hold your breath." And when they embraced, something was wrong. He wanted to laugh—his dick had no more sensation than an icicle. It thawed and slid out of her.

VV pushed him off, rising furiously on an elbow. "Listen to me carefully," she said. "I'm a *woman.* A *mature* woman."

Eli was afraid she was going to cry again. But what she did was take his head in her hands and push it down between her legs. He was exchanging a deep kiss with the complicated mouth of something inhuman. There was an intermittent moan, a loosening in the wind. Then her thighs clutched his head and stoppered his ears, as though he had dived deep into a silent sea.

SEVEN

In this kitchen, Jerry Hook was thinking, so much had happened that was harmless. He could remember midnights here, propping Eli's apple head while Helen fixed a nippled bottle. Now he felt numb as a thumb he'd just seen himself smash with a hammer. The coming pain was certain, and wouldn't hurry.

"In that case," he finally told Helen, "we need to make a decision. We're too old. I'm old." In twenty years, when a baby would be Eli's age, Marigolde would be a crone and he'd be petering out: as old as Helen's father had lived to be. He should inform her immediately that she'd be raising it herself. But he knew that Helen would nod at once, as though she'd expected exactly this, and Hook despaired, beaten by her readiness to suffer.

"Don't show me that face," she said. "It wasn't my idea." She rose, not looking pregnant at all, and carried their plates to the sink. "Anyway, we don't have to decide today."

Hook knew the decision was made. He had already

lost. The rest was pretense. "Sure," he said, "plenty of time." As a child, he'd hated playing out a game with his side hopelessly behind. There seemed to be a rule, strange as the law against suicide, that you couldn't quit, simply quit, just quit and go home.

In their busiest season—requeening and harvesting, extracting and bottling—she helped with everything. As they arrived to harvest honey from the hives at Marigolde's, Helen asked him, "What's this?"

Dozens of cars were there, dented and sagging, starred with rust where rivets had once held strips of chrome. They filled the driveway. Tilting as though they'd begun to melt, they lined the humpbacked road's sloping shoulder of gravel and weed.

"The Smalls," he said. "Something's up."

"Let's come back later."

But as Hook restarted the truck, the front door opened. Marigolde's family was coming down the steps—he saw her brother Vic and Aunt Grace, her Uncle Mike and sister Carolyn, her huge-armed mother. Her father appeared, his U of white hair clasping a scalp that looked shoe-polished. He wore a tight white T-shirt, his belly round and proud. They waved to Hook, yelled "How's it going?", but when they saw that Helen was with him they didn't approach. One by one they swung out into the road, pulling away with a pounding of mufflers and clouds of smoke.

Hook turned off his ignition. Marigolde had seen them and was waving to come in. At the door, the women kissed, which pained him. Because he was sleeping with them both, their embrace seemed perverse. His wife and former wife were nearly friends. Sometimes he imagined them discussing him, even intimate matters. He moistened a fingertip and, where the wallpaper was peeling, tried to press it back down.

"It's Ken," Marigolde told him. "He was arrested last night. He got drunk and borrowed someone's car. We just put together bail."

Hook tugged out his wallet, but Marigolde closed his fingers around it. No matter what Hook thought of him, he knew jail was wrong for Ken. Even if he was guilty, he was innocent. "Bad apple," he explained to Helen. "Always in trouble."

"I'm sorry for him," Marigolde said. "We make fun of Ken because he's dumb. He only wants everyone to like him."

If they had been alone, Hook would have disputed that. But all he could do now was go outside and unload his young queens from the truck. He requeened annually, though Helen's father had worked his queens for two or even three seasons. The business had grown too tough to risk a weakening queen. He puffed smoke into the first hive and opened it carefully: the old queen, swollen with eggs, was there on the center frame. He crushed her against the new queen's cage. Helen and Marigolde came out of the house, descending the lawn side by side in their veils.

"We'd need a room," Helen said. It was mid-afternoon. They were harvesting from the hives in Woody's orchards. "The one next to Eli's." The bees followed in angry streamers as Hook and Helen stacked the white boxes, heavy with honey, in the bed of the truck.

"It's full of junk."

"That could go down to the cellar."

"I just brought it up from the cellar," Hook said, though he had done this at least ten years ago. Stuck in a smear of honey, still alive, a bee was glued between two boxes. He freed her and set her down for her sisters to lick clean.

Back at the honey house, they unloaded the truck. Helen drew the laden frames out of the boxes, handing them to Hook, who sliced off the cells' caps and slid the frames into the extractor. The machine's whir and rattle made them cover their ears. With Helen's father's home-built system of chains and pulleys, Hook raised buckets of extracted honey ceilingward. He had to mount a shaky ladder to tip them into the tank. Big modern honey men, Woody had said sadly, would laugh themselves to death.

While Hook reloaded the extractor, Helen dragged over cartons of jars and started filling them from the tap. Hook shook his head at the color. Less clover, more sumac, darker every year. It was the destruction of meadows, the fault of people like Mangiacapra. He felt caught by a fatal tide. Though Woody had dumped Uncle Seth's Pure Organic Honey, beachheads of Seth's confident symbol were widening on supermarket shelves. Helen caught his eye, and he punched the extractor back on.

"You don't want to talk about this," she said when the noise stopped.

"Maybe if our first had turned out better." Helplessly, Hook thought of times when there had been hope, or had seemed to be: Eli hugging him around the leg, squeezing hard, pressing with his cheek, while Hook dropped a hand to the back of his neck, yoking it with thumb and forefinger, feeling his son's thinness with an ineradicable astonishment.

They were back in the truck, on their way to harvest a final load, when she said, "I know what you want me to do."

He felt, as he turned off Deer Hill Road, onto the trail through the apple trees, that she was putting it somehow unfairly. They bucked over a rut and she grabbed the dash, already protecting her womb. "Don't think about me," he said. "Think about Eli. He'd never come home. Never," he said, certain of it. To Eli, a baby would be obscene.

"Then bring him home first. Go and talk to him, Jerry."

"I'll try." Hook knew he'd have to. So far, he'd done nothing but drive past Cyril's house at night, hoping to spot Eli but afraid to be seen himself: they'd think he was planning something. He'd coasted by Virginia Victor's too, an apartment complex glittering with indistinguishable windows. A better father, he felt, would know exactly how to proceed. Waiting to fall asleep each night, he'd imagined himself seated in Cyril's living room, speaking persuasively, Eli and Cyril nodding, though Hook could never actually hear the words coming out of his mouth.

"Woody will go with you," she said. "He'd love it. Just don't let him bring a gun."

Then they drove without speaking, until Helen said, "We'll think about it. The way I was brought up, you don't throw out what can perfectly well be saved."

Though this made him grind his teeth—it wasn't a matter of thrift!—Hook saw that he'd been making the same mistake. Like her, he had fought to save too much. When he tried to picture her and Eli living without him, all he saw were bulldozers, leveling these trees, plowing out streets that Mangiacapra, embracing his wife in bed, must already have christened in his unstoppable mind. But as Eli had used to say, *que será, será.*

Where a stand of hives backed against the high school athletic field, Hook was surprised to come upon his brother-in-law's truck. He and Helen parked next to it. A moment later Woody himself appeared, walking toward them quickly. "What's doing?" Hook called.

"It's a disaster," Woody said.

"What?"

"They burned your hives. Those punks."

Hook and Helen looked at each other, and he felt their hands touch. "I called Pinhead," Woody said. "I tried you, but no answer."

Hook trotted forward and stopped. Precisely where his hives had been were mounds of ash and blackened wood, still popping as they cooled. Charred combs lay broken, wax twisted like taffy, honey streaked everywhere. Now he smelled it: a dead fireplace, mixed with a head-filling sweetness.

Helen had moved past him and was searching the ashes with a stick. Twenty hives. A ton of honey, Hook judged. A million bees. He pictured them as the heat rose: nurse bees checking the brood cells, queens kept from their laying as protective knots thickened around them. Workers at the entrances, fanning their wings to lower the heat, hanging there and fanning until they caught fire. Because bees obeyed instinct, Hook wouldn't credit them with virtue. He wept in spite of that, even if they could no more be brave than the cells of his own body.

"Don't worry," said Woody. "We'll get them."

"We'll report it," Hook said, "but we won't get them." He couldn't stop counting the neatly spaced mounds. The scene was peaceful. Boy Scouts might have camped here and gone on.

Hunched, inspecting the ground, Helen was moving away, onto the athletic field. Close beside him, Woody spoke. At first Hook didn't understand. He felt dazed, like the surviving bees that buzzed, puzzled, above where their hives had been. He knew they would search until they fell out of the air. Woody's words were strange: *buy you out,* he was saying, his voice soft, *anytime you want.* Hook nodded and struggled to think. It seemed magical, this burning. He tried to remember whether he'd heard Woody's dogs bark last night. "You consider it." Woody squeezed the back of his arm. "You let me know."

"I appreciate that. Tell me something."

"Far as price, we can get an appraisal."

"Last night. Were the dogs out?"

"They aren't trained as guards."

Helen came back, holding something charred, a strip of cloth. "Gasoline." She held it out to be sniffed. "They went down the line with a match and ran like hell." She led Hook and Woody onto the field, pointing out tracks. Where the motorcycles had parked and later spun away, fresh wallows remained, pawed from the earth.

Finally she straightened, shaking her head confusedly. "I've got to make dinner." Hook saw with surprise that the afternoon was drawing down. "Jerry has a doctor's appointment."

He had forgotten it. He was going in to see about his dizzy spells. "We'll pick something up," he said. "You're not cooking tonight."

"Did you ask Woody? About going with you?"

And he'd forgotten that too. Only Helen kept first things first. "To Cyril's," he said. "I thought we might drive over."

"Good." Woody smiled grimly. "I need that."

Back in the truck, Hook and Helen rode in silence, past the Booth estate, past the country club and Paradise Green. Hook felt his mind start to rotate, as it liked to do when he was driving—spiral inward until his destination appeared in his windshield, sudden as a transmission by satellite. A thought persisted, though: it was possible that Woody had burned the hives himself. That would account for the dogs' not barking. Already Hook was half convinced. Woody had done it to make him sell.

Then, paused at a traffic light, he had an even worse thought: that Woody meant to buy him out in order to sell the combined acreage to Mangiacapra. He'd get a far better price for the whole parcel than he would with Hook's few acres stuck in his frontage, obstructing roads, blocking sewers and power lines. Maybe Woody had been eager to sell all along, in spite of his remarks about Mangiacapra, and had only been waiting to get his hands on Hook's property first. He knew Woody hadn't made those motorcycle tracks. Hook tried to stop himself there. But he could feel the idea of Woody's betrayal growing comfortable, turning in his mind, making a familiar place for itself, like an animal settling down in the grass.

When they arrived home with fried chicken and a quart of ice cream, a police car was parked in front of their house. Pinhead Sherman arose from the porch steps. Distantly related to Hook, he'd been a legend to South End kids, glorious as a Stratford High athlete. A few days earlier he had agreed to learn what he could about Cyril. "Sorry about your hives," he said.

Then he told them, "Smells good. No, you enjoy your meal. I'll just visit awhile." But when they were all seated at the table, Helen put a plate before him. Each time he chose a piece of chicken, Pinhead peered into the box carefully to show that he was leaving the plumpest.

"I looked back at where it happened." He licked his fingers, wiped them on a napkin. Then he took out notebook and pen, asking about estimated value. As he wrote, his lips moved. He'd joined the cops, people said, to escape his sports nickname, but it hadn't worked. "Hear anything about Eli?"

"He hasn't called," Hook said. "Hasn't written."

Helen said, "I think he's been brainwashed."

"Did he ever have a fondness for fires?"

Helen was furious, Hook saw, and he told her Pinhead had to ask that. "We figure it was the Zombies."

Pinhead nodded. "Here's what I found on that guy. Nothing but motor vehicle violations. His legal name"—he licked the tip of a long finger to page through his notebook—"is James Martin Birmingham. The Bridgeport cops suspect he torched a drunk last winter, down by the railroad station."

"Torched?" said Helen.

"They couldn't prove it."

"What else have you got?" Hook asked. "Proven or unproven."

Pinhead slapped his notebook shut. "Incident in a men's room."

"Rape?"

"You don't want to hear about it. Something closer to castration."

Hook took Helen's hand, pushing his plate of chicken bones aside, and then put both his arms around her. Though he saw on the kitchen clock how late it was getting, he thought he'd hold her just like this—it felt safe—and not move at all.

"Never proven," Pinhead said. "The cops can't do a thing to him, unless they do it in street clothes. Which they might. This is the kind of guy they hate."

Ever since he'd made the appointment, Hook had half-expected to learn on this circled date that his condition was fatal. But Dr. Zimanski, bifocaled and bald, was chatting sociably as he examined him, showing no concern and paying, Hook felt, no great attention. When Hook described his dizzy spells, Zimanski didn't take notes, only sat and looked and nodded, fingers laced across his fly. During the electrocardiogram he spoke of his grandchildren. Tugging on a rubber glove, he joked about his wife's bad cooking. "Just relax," he told Hook. "Draw your knee up to your chest." He'd been their family doctor for years, but now he'd grown old, perhaps negligent.

So when the examination was done, Hook buttoning his cuffs, and the time had come for Zimanski to extend a freshly washed hand and say "I want you back in a year," Hook was astonished to be told instead that he ought to have a pacemaker. He couldn't believe he'd heard it right: a cardiac pacemaker.

"For my heart? Inside my chest?" He wanted to laugh. A retired priest he knew, eighty and frail, had a pacemaker. Supreme Court justices got them. But had anybody from the South End ever had one?

"Your heart's strong," Zimanski said. "Its internal communications are getting"—he paused—"iffy. The chambers are fine, but your ventricle's beginning to miss signals. How'd you like to have it done in the next couple of weeks?"

Hook felt a fear he couldn't name. Not that his heart was sick—it still felt fine—and not of the surgery itself. He didn't object to having machinery sewn into him. He trusted science: as a bee man, he was a scientist himself. But a mechanical rhythm in his heart would change him. It would change the way he touched things. He thought the bees would know.

"This is local anesthesia only, less discomfort than a toothache. You'll be in the hospital forty-eight hours, and your health insurance will pay." First, Zimanski said, he'd strap on a monitor that Hook would wear for a day. Then they'd be ready anytime he was. The sooner the better. "Suppose you faint behind the wheel? With this device, that can't happen. You're basically in wonderful health. This will make you perfect."

Hook said he wanted to think about it. But then, imagining the drive home, he immediately pictured himself passing out, an eighteen-wheeler head-on. He said okay. Zimanski shook his hand, looking relieved. Hook knew he was lucky; suppose it had been a brain tumor? Still, the knowledge that he was fixable—far better than that, perfectible—left him lonely. There had been comfort in the secret idea that he was dying, an idea never believed but always kept ready to believe. It had been a companion, like money in the bank.

"One more thing. One question. This isn't related, except, well—" Hook hesitated, smiling. "We're thinking of having another child, Helen and I. Any reason why we shouldn't? If I have a pacemaker? And she's forty."

"I'd hesitate to advise it. Personally I would be dubious."

"I understand. Because of the risks? Birth defects?"

"No, I'm thinking of your lives generally, your ease and comfort."

"And Helen's health?"

"That's not my department. But judging by appearances—" Zimanski flourished his hands in the air, sculpting a slim waist, and left it admiringly at that.

Outside, it had grown dark. Hook drove home slowly. His life was going to be scientifically extended, which should bring him joy. What he felt instead was obligation inexplicably laced with anger. Six months left to live he could simply have let pass. But a man with many years to go had an irresistible duty. As a matter purely of stewardship—as a responsibility he no longer wanted—a life that long needed to be made good.

The moon had risen when his brother-in-law picked him up in the Cadillac. Speeding along the Connecticut Turnpike into Bridgeport, Woody said to let him handle it—this type of gent responded to firmness. They parked around the corner from Cyril's address and walked up to the door, Woody grinding his right fist into his left palm.

"Listen," Hook said. "If Eli's here, all I want is a chance to talk to him. Don't start a fight."

Woody didn't reply. He seemed to be trying to crush Cyril's doorbell, leaning heavily into his forefinger. After several long rings, with pauses that grew shorter, he cursed and began to knock loudly.

It was then that Hook noticed what looked like a marble embedded in the door and realized it was a viewing hole. He touched Woody's arm and pointed, imagining the balloon of fingertip and rubber-band arm that anyone peering through would see.

As he pointed, the door began to open. It stopped at an inch, tethered there by a brass chain. In the slit was a section of face, pale skin, high forehead. "Birmingham?" Woody demanded. The man said nothing. "I'm Underwood. This is Mr. Hook. Open the door."

"Show me your identification."

Woody started to reach for his wallet. Then he said, "Screw that."

The door closed. Hook grabbed Woody's arm just as he was about to start pounding. "Mr. Birmingham," he called. "Is Eli there?"

The door opened again to the length of its chain. "He's working tonight. You want to leave a message?"

"No, I want to talk to you. May we come in?"

Woody put his face close to the slit. "You haven't got the balls to open this door."

It clicked shut. Then metal slid against metal. The door sprang away—Cyril had pulled while Woody was pushing. They were in a narrow hall. Overhead a naked bulb swung on a cord, making their shadows pivot and reach. Before them, stairs ascended to the second floor. Cyril filled the stairway—having seen only an inch of him, Hook was astonished at his breadth. His height seemed tremendous as he loomed on the steps above them.

"Watch it," Woody said, "he's armed." And then Hook saw the impossibly long blade in Cyril's hands. A machete?

But Cyril seemed calm. "I haven't got the—what?" He swayed from one foot to the other.

Woody moved to the center of the hall, shielding Hook behind him. Hook was amazed at his unthinking, dog-like bravery. "Time's up," Woody said. "We're taking him back."

"His mother and I want Eli home," Hook said, in what he hoped was a more reasonable voice. Then, to his surprise and shame, he felt himself beginning to cry.

"I'll give him the message," Cyril said, "but he won't come. Not until he knows who he is." Grinning, he added, "Or at least what sex."

Hook couldn't remember, afterward, how he'd gotten by Woody. His first clear impression was of Cyril overturned, wriggling on the steps like a beetle. Then he felt himself flying backward. As Cyril struggled to his feet, raising the machete, Woody pulled him out the door, slamming it, and down the steps.

They stopped under a street light. "Let's see that hand," Woody panted. Hook, puzzled, held out both of them. Blood was oozing from a slash across his left palm.

"Wiggle your fingers," Woody said. "Good. Better wrap it in this." He gave Hook a handkerchief. "What a shot, Red. Right in the mouth. Jesus." Hook was amazed—he couldn't remember hitting Cyril at all.

Yet by the time they got home, Woody had described it to him so many times that—though they hadn't accomplished what they'd come for—Hook could feel himself growing proud. His hand hurt, but the bleeding had nearly stopped. Suddenly he remembered his heart, palmed his chest, felt nothing. How would he fight Cyril after his heart was wired and reined?

"Good job for a couple of old guys," Woody said, letting him out, squeezing his shoulder. "Can you make it inside okay?"

He drove off with a tap of his horn and a spray of gravel. Hook stood there until he was gone, and the mild night quiet. Then he crunched down the gravel drive, past his nursery hives, toward the house's lit windows. On such a still night the bees would be thickening the last of their nectar, ripening it to be capped for winter food. He thought of them in every hive, hugging the comb, beating the air with invisible wings, drying the drops that other bees held out on microscopic tongues.

For the first time, the idea of this brilliant industry frightened him. Because none of it was for themselves, all of it was for their race. For grubs asleep in sealed cells, and next year's generation in the egg.

EIGHT

It's his favorite saying. "As long as you live," Cyril always tells us, "you keep learning." But tonight he sighs and adds, "There's not much more I can teach you. Now I'll show you how I teach myself."

An hour ago I ate whale with Pal and Mondo. Chemicals are terrific for them, Cyril says. For me, stupid. Same as for him. Our natures are higher than theirs. But I've been unwrapping something, layer after layer—that's how I explained it, while he just kept looking sad—until I can't go any deeper without a blade. Virginia is furious. She didn't want me to take the pill either.

"Astral travel," Cyril says, "is basically simple. Besides your physical body, you have an astral body. It can move in space and time, which also exist on the astral plane. The astral plane. Now what's that." He leans forward, elbows on knees, palms kissing, eyes tacking us all into place. He says it's an ocean, the astral plane. All through space. All through time. "Does that concept melt too fast? Andrea? Mr. June?"

They're the newest in the group and hardly ever speak.

Andrea's a nice girl. She writes poems. Once Cyril told her to read them aloud. But she was shy and finally just handed one around, a poem about her being crushed and burned. It made me sorry for her, even though Virginia said later, when we were in bed, that the imagery was entirely sexual and rather forced.

"No," says Mr. June, "I think I've got it." June claims he drives a bus. But Cyril pointed out to me, grabbing my wrists with his own cab-driver hands so I felt their roughness, that June's hands aren't calloused from steering. "An ocean," June says, but I know he isn't seeing anything.

"Every night," Cyril says, "you travel in your astral body. It happens in your dreams. You can do it when you're awake, too."

His voice is smoother than natural—glass washed up on shore. "I'm ready, man," Mondo says. The Holy Father closes his eyes and nods. Virginia is smiling. Sometimes I wonder if she believes any of this.

First Cyril makes us relax, one muscle group at a time. "Now," he says, "escape from your body. There's no way in the world it can hold you. You're expanding. Ever make bread? You're bread dough. You're swelling in every direction."

He gives a long puff, like somebody blowing up a beachball. "Sliding out through the toes. A bubble at the elbow. Feel it?"

And I do. In my head, a sponge is filling with warm liquid. My hands are huge. In a minute I'm leaking out everywhere. I feel as light as though I haven't eaten in weeks. "Okay, slowly." Cyril inflates the beachball again, long and deep. "You just ooze. You emanate in every direction." He waits a long time. Then he says, "You are now in your astral body."

"But don't forget where you put your physical body," Virginia says, serious-joking.

Cyril says the first thing to learn, now that we're in our astral bodies, is how to travel through space. "Picture yourself outdoors. Somewhere familiar." It's the front yard of my parents' house. When I turn around, my father is behind the living-room window, leaning on the sill, showing me the blue veins in his wrists. "Rise," Cyril says. "Rise. It's in your power. Rise twelve inches."

Pal grunts. Mondo grunts. "Shut up if you can't do it," Cyril says—the first time he's ever told them not to be idiots. "Higher now. Three feet up, and then look down." When I do, I'm dizzy, it's like being on stilts. "Go right up to a hundred feet," Cyril says, "and remember, you're perfectly safe."

What I notice right away are the wind and the brightness, no shade anywhere. I see Deer Hill Road, winding between the orchards and the half-built Mangiacapra project. Woody's house reflects the sun like a signal fire off its kitchen skylight. I can see the river, widening into the Sound, and one of those houses next to the river is Marigolde's, where my father goes to screw her. His face is the size of a fingertip, pressed against our front window, pointing up at me.

"An exercise," Cyril says. "Let it become night. A simple exercise in time. Relax and enjoy the sunset."

I do it, but a little wrong. One blast of pink and then it's dark and cold. Cars on the Merritt Parkway push intersecting cones of light, and my parents' windows throw a fuzzy halo. Then the house goes black. The stars wheel above me. Out of Milford, beyond the river, the white moon jumps into the sky.

Now I understand what Cyril meant about the whale. How will I know later if this is real? It feels too safe to be anything but a daydream. All I need to do is tap the air with my soles, every few seconds, to stay in place, bobbing in the wind. The moon, all pits and scars, swings by. When I see the east getting bright, that seems like something I can control. But there's a trick, a twisting thing I need to do with my jaw. I catch the moon, halved at the horizon, and pull it back up as the east goes dark again.

"The seasons," Cyril says. I hear him, down on the earth. "Go through the year," he tells me through earphones.

I keep it night, with the moon full. When the snow begins to fall I'm afraid it will ride me to the ground, but it just sifts through my astral body. There's dripping from the rain gutters, tremendous dripping in the orchards, and the trees bush out under the moon. The wind warms. I can smell blossoms, then honey. The nursery hives stand in rows, gravestones in the moonlight. Next the trees are bare again. Smoke curls from my parents' chimney.

Cyril is having transmission problems. I watch his mouth to get the words. We're moving millions of miles, out to a fixed point in space. He says our planet is spinning faster and faster around the sun. Now I have to paddle with my hands or I turn and turn, like a worm on a hook. The earth whizzes away from me, whips around the sun and comes whirling back and away and back so fast it blurs like the spokes of a bicycle wheel.

"Okay, when you return to earth, where are you?"

"The future," Pal says sweetly, trying to make up for getting Cyril mad before.

"If anything," the Holy Father says, "it would have to be the past." His body waves gently, graceful as seaweed. "You're following the earth's orbit backwards. It's the observer who's speeding up."

"Do you know who you were?"

It's a seashore. Though now I'm only as high as the tops of the palm trees, I can see that this is an island. It's little, like someone's present, centered for wrapping in wrinkled blue. Naked on the beach is the boy I saw in the book of my life. He's nothing like me— smaller, darker. But the wet sand crunches under my heels, and I am him. I'm after something, stepping into the cold foam, a thing that gleams and bobs sideways, wading toward it, clawing water, toes stretching to dance the pebbly shifting bottom. Up where the dry sand burns my knees, I tug out the salty cork with my teeth. There's a piece of paper. The handwriting is hard, but I have time.

"Besides myself," Cyril says, "you're the only one who experienced this. You know that?" His hand is warm on my knee.

When I open my eyes, he and I are alone. I can see everyone else through a doorway, standing around a table. "Break time," Cyril says. "Afterwards, Virginia has a surprise for us."

"I was reading something," I tell him.

"Good," he says, "that's good. Is it something you can finish later?"

I fold the message and slide it into my hip pocket. He gives me a hand up out of my chair, and I follow him into the dining room.

• • •

We started having breaks, with wine and cheese, when Cyril raised the weekly contribution from two dollars to five. Pal said, "Profit for the Bull, Chianti's three forty-nine a gallon," but he didn't really care. "We're telling him, please fuck me." He turned around, sticking out his skinny ass. "We're backing up and dropping our pants and saying oh please, stick it in right here. So he does it. And he should."

Standing up cleared my head. Voices are sculpted in the air. When I look across at Virginia, talking to the Holy Father, I can see the pores of her skin. I don't know what surprise she has, and I'm sad she never told me, even holding each other in bed. Cyril gets down on his hands and knees. He crawls along the floor into the kitchen and makes a quick grab in the corner. Cricket: he shows it around, jumping legs pinched in his fingers, before he feeds it to his snakes. "How's your trip," Pal asks, and I tell him mediocre. His is paranoid, he says, a little proudly. "Try the cheese." He points. Mondo is sitting cross-legged under the table, naked to the waist, a piece of cheese in each hand. When he sees me looking, he holds some out. It tastes the way Vaseline would taste, if Vaseline tasted good.

Then we're all moving back to the living room. "What'd you lose?" Cyril asks me. I realize I've been searching my pockets, and when I remember what I thought I put there, I feel stupid.

Back in our chairs, Virginia distributes stapled copies of something typed. "You should each have ten pages," she says, "seven of text, two of footnotes. Plus the bibliography." At the top of the first page there's a title. GENETIC "It's for a scholarly journal, so it's technical in spots. I'll read it aloud and try to untangle the cruxes. Then I'll ask for your input."

GENETIC AND EPIDEMIOLOGICAL
ELEMENTS IN "REINCARNATION"

What follows is a hypothesis, consistent with the current state "state of scientific knowledge," she reads, "that will offer a rational basis for validating some of the commonly"

I realize she's been working on this, must have been, for weeks. And never asked for my input. She won't discuss reincarnation when we're alone. Any more than when we're here she seems to know we ever spend the night together. How can she change like that? I thought we'd be intimate. But a lot of the time we're actors. She likes it if one of us wears clothes, she tells me to be angry or scared, she'll lie back and fold her arms—"Astonish me," she'll say. She says, "I want you to be happy," but I'm nervous when I come to bed. If I ask about her cancer, she laughs, and after a while she starts shouting. She doesn't have it, her health is perfect, so why am I frightening her, why do I want to think she's dying? "You *are* a macabre child." But it's just an idea—to me, it shows her courage. In the morning her pillow is sketched with curling strokes of hair, and I wonder if she's losing it from chemotherapy. Sometimes we'll lie in bed with glasses of wine and she'll whip out her little magnetic chessboard. We work on openings and end-games. She loves to teach, and I keep nodding, even when I don't understand, so she'll keep feeling good.

consider reincarnatability a recessive trait. That isn't where she is: "Immunity would be genetically dominant," she's reading. She's gotten way ahead of me. *But it is not the reincarnation itself that is inherited; it is the reincarnatability. To bring this potentiality to realization, an* I turn a page. *that the agent is a virus. Its vector*

"But immune persons," she reads, and then, dropping her pitch, interrupts herself—"which we've been calling grubs"—Pal snorts—"could have susceptible children. It would appear that our species, *Homo sapiens,* includes two closely related, mutually fertile subspecies."

I've never been so aware of her speech—"subspecies" is full of whistles. "That's racist," says the Holy Father. She asks if everyone will hold their questions until the end. *The genetic mechanism is susceptibility to the virus,* it says, but she's reading, "One, the numerically superior, lacks a soul," and she interrupts herself again—"for lack of a better word. Spirit. Call it what you will. You see the terminological swamp I'm in."

modification within its host, encoding experience

"We *all* have souls," says the Holy Father.

"Let her finish," Cyril says, and Pal echoes him, in the same voice of warning.

"The viruses are immensely long-lived. It would be possible for you to be Aristotle and for me to be Plato. But statistically, and here please look at footnote three, the tables for time and distance." I can't find them in the slithery pages. When I lean to one side to put the typescript under my chair, weights roll in my head and I catch myself with my palm on the floor. I straighten up and the weights roll back, settling halfway into holes, like the chrome ball bearings in a puzzle I had when I was little. My crossed legs touch each other strangely, unfamiliar and familiar, legs in translation.

"Thus we see that there is neither pre-existence nor re-existence. Present lives are primary, past lives are acquired, exactly the opposite of what is usually assumed. They are accidentally acquired by the small minority of persons genetically susceptible to the operative agent. Let me only say in conclusion that science will someday smile, I trust tolerantly, at this first attempt, and regard my virus as a metaphor for agents we can't presently detect."

I'm anesthetized all over. I've never felt so safe in my life. If anything tries to hurt me, I'll squirt to the side like a watermelon seed. Cyril is at the blackboard. "I'm very impressed with Virginia's theory."

"Hypothesis," she says.

"Because here's what comes right out of it. You start by recognizing that it's us, the minority, who are fully alive." He writes on the board:

FULLY ALIVE

"And grubs—" He writes that down too, at an angle.

FULLY ALIVE

"—grubs aren't. We can call ourselves humans."

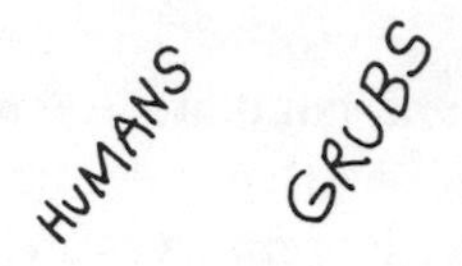

FULLY ALIVE

I've never seen anything like this. I laugh or have a thought of laughing, a memory or foreknowledge of it, but Cyril doesn't look up. He's still writing.

	HUMANS	GRUBS
DANGEROUS		
FULLY ALIVE		

"The tissue is there," he says, "but not the spirit. As Virginia pointed out, no soul. You and I are the ones they'll put in Newtown," his chalk clicks angrily, "and sever our pre-frontal lobes."

	HUMANS	GRUBS
DANGEROUS	NO	YES
FULLY ALIVE	YES	NO

I'm trying to keep this forever, the way everything fits. Not just ideas. How the wall and ceiling meet at a segment of line.

Local. One line. One segment of one line. Making infinity wait outside.

"—androids," Cyril says.

"Unplug them," Pal says. "Abort them."

"You'd keep some as breeding stock," Cyril explains. "Anyhow, it'd be impossible to get them all. Right, Virginia? According to your theory?"

"Hypothesis. Someone should see if Eli's okay."

I open my eyes so they'll know that I am. Andrea is coming across the room. She puts her hands on my shoulders and looks into my face. Cyril is rubbing his fingers together, trying to get rid of the chalk. He's drawn lines and cross-hatching.

	HUMANS	GRUBS
DANGEROUS	NO	YES
FULLY ALIVE	YES	NO

"I don't mean," he says, "mass pigicide. I'm talking about a symbolic act. Not any specific result at all. You never control results."

My eyes have to close again. The Holy Father is saying something angry. Pal speaks and Cyril speaks and Mondo says, "Poison, man. Hypnotic *poison*." Pal says something and there's laughter that goes on as long as a symphony.

"The chair," Cyril says, "is ready to receive nominations."

If the exact words were spoken, I missed them. But I know what he means—killing my father. I've made myself think about that, sometimes, just so I can hate myself enough to not think about it for another month or week. Hearing him chosen now is weird, as though Cyril knows what I need better than I ever did. I can't do it, though. It's not like swatting flies or putting a cat in the microwave. I think about him every time I open Cyril's refrigerator. Inside, there's Deer Hill Honey. I never told Cyril that he's got my father's brand. We're eating him all the time, spread on toast, stirred into tea.

When I look again, the Holy Father is standing. He says, "That's it for me," and walks to the door.

"What's the matter?" Cyril says. "We're discussing events on the astral plane. Didn't you get that?"

"No," the Holy Father says. "I think you should stop it right now." Then there's no sound except his feet trotting downstairs.

Cyril goes to the window. "That's our spy," he says. Pal says, in his King of the Jungle voice, "*Eat him, my brothers.*" He and Mondo start chanting it. The meeting is breaking up. By the door, Mr. June is helping Virginia with her coat. Her hands go into the armhole mouths. She points her chin at me and says something to Cyril.

"I'll clean up," he says when we're alone. I close my eyes and am back on the lion-colored sand, running into the waves for something that gleams and bobs. Later, I notice Cyril on the floor in front of me, kneeling close, hunched over. My pants are open. His eyes roll up at me.

Standing is easier than I expected. I go into my room and shut the door. He opens it and says, "I'll miss you, but you better move out of here."

"Okay." I want to stay, though. Not only for myself—for him. Being alone scares him. I know that. He knows I know.

"If you come back, you understand the terms."

I think of my father lying in blood on the bathroom floor. I picture him in pieces on the soaking bed.

"Would it cost you a lot?"

Then I understand. It's backwards. Good people don't think they're good. A sacrifice that I can afford isn't a sacrifice. If I don't know why I have to do it, my ignorance is the reason. It's backwards only for a minute—until I can hold it in my mind one certain way.

NINE

"Red, you look sick. Relax! No harm done."

The lonely hole, almost in the middle of Woody's plate-glass window, reminds me of a navel. I touch the puncture where the lead slug buried itself in plasterboard and insulation. Then I look back at the window, wondering why the whole sheet didn't shatter. Seeing the bullet's trajectory—what its indifference would do to a solved puzzle of belly organs—makes me spread my hands across my shirt buttons.

"We were asleep," Woody says. "I ran through the house, I thought we had a burglar. Three a.m. Then I saw the twenty-two was gone." Curving a shoulder, tucking an elbow, he shows me how he rolled to the floor and crawled for his thirty-thirty. He's still frightened, I can feel it. But Woody hates cowards. He orders me to keep this quiet.

"He came in later and said"—Woody makes innocent eyes—"Dad, what happened to the wall? I twisted his arm off. He'd hidden the gun in the woodpile."

Disgusted, he jerks his chin at the ceiling. Pal is upstairs in his room. "What does he need, a psychiatrist?" But I see Woody bulging with love, the same as when our boys were little. I practically smell that love, as though some fatherly gland has been squeezed. "They're the master race, you know? They hope to screw up our systems and exterminate us. Make us die from overeating. Take away our interest in sex. Not mine, buddy!" When Woody is like this, he just gets worse if you argue. "Change our body scent, is their theory. Make it so males will only mate with males. Or immature females, or pregnant ones."

"Your boy's got an imagination," I tell him. "Calm down. They can't do any of those things." He's made me think of my pregnant wife.

"Meantime, the cops are holding their pricks." He comes up close and says softly, "Before you have your operation, let's go back and really beat the shit out of him." I see us with our boys' old baseball bats, climbing Cyril's steps. We should talk to the cops, I say. But Woody doesn't trust the cops. "I trust myself," he says. "That's who I trust. Myself and you."

Driving away, I put a hand on my heart. In a week I'll have a power plant sewn into me. Now that seems a foolish decision: hide from death and you become a target. All Pal wanted to shoot was a window—he knows his parents sleep at the other end of the house—so why am I hunching down in my seat? The posture feels ridiculous, and it takes me the whole ride home to force myself, a little at a time, to straighten up.

• • •

Trimester is a word we haven't used. When I was a kid, words would wait, like water in the pipes. But these days there are words that frighten me—words that push to be actual things. Confident words that keep moving forward, as though they were the people and not us.

We're working when Helen says it, getting the bees ready for winter. There's been a light frost. Nectar is drying up; all they're bringing in is pollen. We walk down the rows, hefting the colonies to check their stores. "I'm past the first trimester," she says. "But he told me not to consider its viability. Not at my age."

Viability I know about. I know it in the grub, I know it in the egg. Lifting, I find a hive that's light—a weak colony that will probably starve—not viable—and put a bottle feeder on top. "Then there's no problem."

She doesn't answer. I get my caulking compound from the truck and we go around again, making the hives weather-tight for winter. It's one of those dark afternoons, sheets of lightning without thunder. When we come to the weak colony, I seal its cracks with extra care. Then I narrow its entrance so they can defend their stores against autumn robbers.

"All right," Helen says when we're back in the truck. We're bouncing through the orchards, on our way to the hives at Marigolde's. "Don't look like a martyr, Jerry. You win."

"I win?"

"You win."

But I know her very, very well. I haven't won. Something's missing. We pull onto Deer Hill Road and roll our windows shut. The air is bitter, burning. Off to the left, Mangiacapra's men are laying gleaming black streets.

I can see hundreds of bees raiding the asphalt, picking stickum for winter repairs. One of the workers, leaning on a shovel, suddenly snaps back his head, smacking the air.

I tell her, "This is a good decision. It'll be best."

"I'm glad you're glad." She slides close, bending her knees to miss the gearshift lever. She puts one arm around my shoulders, the other around my chest, and I want to unwrap her. It's what I love from Marigolde, but in Helen it's degrading. "I'm glad," she says. "I love you very much."

"I love you."

"I'd kill for you."

Her arms squeeze, her breath is hot on my neck. I tell her I won't buy it, not like that.

"Listen, Jerry." Finally she lets go. "I'm not easy, I know it. And you're not, but that's my fault, you used to be." I remember meeting her in the library, Helen, nineteen, as vertical as if she kept her character in her bones. "Now I'll do what you want."

Unless I'm careful, my feelings will fool me. Love and tenderness like milk, but the fact that I'm leaving her is part of them. "And forgive me after I'm dead, correct?"

She smiles and says, "Forgiveness is for children. I don't forgive myself. You pay for power."

We've reached Marigolde's. Seeing her is always like I've been granted a concession, some accommodation. I can already feel it start, like a headwind shifting out of my way. But as we pull into her driveway, Marigolde is backing out. "Getting some groceries," she calls, drifting past us in reverse. When I see her framed in her car window, the whites of her eyes, the arcs of her cheekbones, grocery shopping seems joyous. I want to go with her. Buy for a thousand miles of highway, bread and cold cuts, Coke in cans. Get gas, check the tires, stop at the bank. "Hey," she yells. She brakes abruptly: her car sways, her head and body sway. "Guess who came into the office? Somebody loosened his front teeth."

We shut off our engines and get out. "Eli's big friend," she says.

They both know I socked Cyril. I'm embarrassed and proud. "Tell us about him," I say. "What was your impression of the guy?"

"All puffed out, a big ham, he's playing the role, but underneath he's a harmless baby. We get all the characters. He's typical, his mouth is full of instruments and he's flirting with our hygienist."

"Was he talking crazy?"

"She told him he's facing major expense, but he didn't listen. Expense and pain. He just wants them polished up. He thinks he has a killer smile."

I can't help looking at her, trying to see if she's attracted to him. Of course she knows what I'm thinking. "A typical type of patient," she says. She believes it: to a Small, everything's weird, but nothing is weirder than usual. "He admitted he's been in pain for years. He's neglected his mouth. He needs a root canal and a job on his gums."

When I hear this, and picture Cyril gaping in the chair, reclined with a bib around him, hands gripping the armrests, feet wiggling while the drill hums high as a dog whistle, he doesn't seem so dangerous. The man I hit is starting to become a dream. "I guess he didn't mention Eli," Helen says. Marigolde shakes her head.

After she drives away, under clouds packed solid as scoops of chocolate swirl, Helen and I put on our veils. All these hives are good and heavy. There's just the caulking to do, and we work quickly, along two rows. "Jerry," she says. "I know about the window. Violet told me."

I bend to the next hive, feeling caught in a lie. "He wasn't shooting at them." The bees are reducing their population for winter—in front of the entrance, the ground is dotted with dead and dying drones.

"She asked if Eli had a gun. I think I'm scared. Get him back."

"I'll go again." A worker is tugging out another drone, buzzing her wings, the drone struggling.

"Talk to that woman."

"I'll talk to her."

"I couldn't." As though the woman were in her mouth, Helen's lips purse, her cheeks pucker. Then she actually leans to the side, lifts her veil, and spits, something I've never seen her do except into a tissue.

"I can go today," I say. "To her office." According to Pal, Eli is living in her apartment. But I feel as though seeing his life there could kill me. He's not doing this for sex, it isn't that normal. He's too cold to love anyone. I've been driving by her place, and once I saw her leave. I parked, I thought I'd knock on the door. But I was afraid to see whatever he's become.

Up high, thunder hits and rolls. Helen looks at the sky and says, "He didn't take his windbreaker."

It starts to rain and we hurry to finish the last hives. But by the time we're back in the truck, our hats and veils piled on the floor between Helen's feet, the shower is over. Again I want to hunch down—I'm imagining how one bullet through the window could kill us both. When a pickup coming at us flashes its lights and honks, I panic and swerve before I see who it is.

Ken waves. As we pass, I get a good look at him. He's grinning, jabbing a forefinger forward, toward Marigolde's house. "Jackass!" He looks happier, more eager, than I can remember feeling in years.

"What?"

I tell her who it was. "Why's he so persistent? She hates him."

"Maybe she's of two minds."

"Hardly."

"She's been single a long time, you know," Helen says. "Women have needs too."

Most people might say they make a nice-looking couple. But to me, nothing is uglier than the thought of Marigolde with Ken. I can picture him putting his arms around her, his Miller cans crumpled on her bedside table. I can hear his whoop of pleasure. "Oh, come on!"

Helen stares, as if something tiny is crawling on my face. Then I know I've said too much. "She can do better than him, that's all."

"My God," she says slowly. "You want her for yourself. Still."

"Ken's a moron. I don't care how sweet he is. He doesn't deserve to sit in her kitchen and fart up the air."

"Have you been seeing her?"

"*Seeing* her?"

"Well," she says, "I believe you. But I think you have that fantasy, sometimes."

"Does fantasy count?"

"This disappoints me, Jerry. This lowers you in my eyes. It shows you'd rather be a worse person."

And I realize she's right, I would. A far worse person, a terrible person. I look at her. How can she be so smart? As we turn onto Deer Hill Road, she says, "You'd be having an affair now if you thought I wouldn't find out." We're passing the reservoir. Woody's orchards begin. "Or if you thought Eli wouldn't find out. He's the one you love, not me. You want to go? I'll give you three days. Get your things together. I'll stay at my brother's until you're gone."

I'm frightened, she's so far ahead. "I'm not going anywhere. Neither are you."

When we stop, Helen turns to face me. "Please don't explain your feelings. Just let me know your plans."

I've pictured this scene so many times, and always wrong: the wild words I've put in her mouth, the hot tears I've made her cry. I say, "I'm grateful to you. Yes. I'm not sure what I want." I can hear how weak that sounds, and she looks at me with contempt. "One thing at a time, okay? I'll try to get him straightened out. Then we'll see where we find ourselves."

But what's happening now, what starts even before I finish, is terrifying. Helen's face does things I've never seen. She still doesn't cry, but her veins and tendons leap as if she's straining under torture. Her eyes are shut. Her jaw falls open. Her tongue, thick and quivering, fills her mouth like someone stuffed it there to choke her. "All right, then," she says, and what's awful is how close to normal, my old Helen, she can make her voice. "Do it. Straighten him out, Jerry. Straighten him out."

• • •

I wash and change: jacket and tie. Then I drive down Barnum Avenue, past the cemetery, and into Bridgeport to the college. Pulling up in the parking lot, it seems only a day or two since I was here last spring.

And inside, I can't believe it, is the same old guy. Is it the same guy? Instead of the wastebasket of dolls, he's carrying a sign on a pole: THERE IS LIFE BEFORE BIRTH. He sees me coming and twirls it. THERE IS LIFE AFTER DEATH, it says on the reverse. He holds out a blood-red leaflet. I remember those photographs. Without looking, I stick it into my breast pocket, where there's already a little graveyard of shredded tissues, dusty hairy cough drops, a pointless pencil. When I thank the guy he smiles and Godblesses me. "You read that, now."

I remember where her office is. Approaching it, I can picture her face perfectly. She'll recognize me, the mature student—how will I explain that? I decide she won't recognize me, not from half a year ago. I'm bent over in front of her door, trying to read the office hours typed on an index card, when I realize that if she's in there, she'll see me, fuzzy against her frosted window, and just as I'm thinking this she calls, "Who is it?"

In Virginia Victor's hand is a red felt-tip marker. Propped forward on her elbows, she seems surrounded by her desk. There are ragged piles of papers, crooked stacks of books. More books lying open, others spread face down like prisoners of war. She gazes up at me so wearily that the first thing I feel is all wrong—concern, maybe affection. Through oversized glasses, her gray eyes widen.

"Mister—?"

"Hook."

"Mister Hook." She smiles as if she doesn't place the name. But I know she guessed who I am the second she saw me. "Please come in. Shut the door. Sit down."

I do it. I always admire people—like Woody, like Helen—who have that habit of command. My chair is lower than hers. I figure I should start with a compliment, maybe something about her office. But all I say, beginning to sweat, is "Eli's father."

"I inferred that." She smiles again, which makes me hope things aren't too bad. "We've met, I realize. Your slyness hurts me. That charade was manipulative."

"I apologize."

"Manipulative and somehow flirtatious."

Now I'm blushing. "I was afraid—"

"I know you were, I understand. And I understand why you've come today. He's a fine, fine boy."

"A fine boy, he is."

"He's very fine." She smiles encouragingly, as though I'm a student who needs to be coached.

"This," I say, "group. This bunch, this club he's in."

I stop because she's begun to nod, the way a teacher does when you finally get to the point. "Of course. I entirely understand your feelings, which are natural and normal. As it happens, Eli's less active in the group these days."

"Good," I say, before I can think. Then I'm afraid I shouldn't have, maybe she'll be insulted.

She's still nodding. "The group is stimulating, mind you. But often imma-toor. They regard me as their big sister." An extra wrinkle in her smile says it's a compliment she doesn't value.

"Is he okay?"

She touches the fingertips of her two hands together. A spider doing push-ups on a mirror, we called that when I was little.

"I mean feeling okay?"

"Right now he's become withdrawn. That's the way I think I'd put it."

"Withdrawn?"

"I'd say he's sorting things out."

That sounds okay. I picture him sitting in his underwear, on the edge of an unmade bed. Withdrawn? It's his middle name. I see his posture, his expression. "We're worried," I say. "We want him home. We love him." And then, because I hadn't planned to say that, I loosen my tie to breathe.

"Concerned?" She looks as though she doesn't believe it.

"We're completely in the dark. It sounds angry, this outfit. The crowd he's with. Dangerous. We're afraid it's dangerous for him."

She cocks her head.

"Hostile," I try. "A hostile situation."

"Bitter? Hostile?"

"Yes."

"Antisocial?"

"Yes. Yes."

She frowns, making the mirrored spider again. I watch it slowly stretch and hump. "Society is in no danger. Rather, society is a danger to the group."

"That's it, that's what we're worried about."

Her chair is the swiveling kind, and now she begins to swing slowly from side to side. She's become a pendulum, ticking off the time until I leave. It's more and more maddening. "Maybe I've said all I can without invading Eli's privacy. I'll just add that I know he loves his parents very much. A reunion would be good for him."

"Then why is he staying away?" From how I'm breathing, I can tell that I'm ready to pop. But instead I try to sound defeated. Something tells me that's her weakness—she'll be generous once she thinks she has you. "Can't he sort things out pretty quick? If he's not home for Thanksgiving we'll feel terrible. Please tell him."

"He'll come," she says. "Generally he listens to me. Eli's a boy who's had a rough time, and he doesn't trust easily. He's learned to see me as a surrogate mother."

That insolent remark shows me how much I love my wife. Horribly, there *is* a resemblance—not in features, but some of her expressions are Helen's. When she sits there smiling at the end of her speech, swiveling back and forth—sliding down in her chair in a manner that's supposed to be sexy—it makes me furious. Then I feel what she's putting him through.

"All right," I say. "Here's a fact. Can we start with a fact? Eli's living with you. Isn't he?"

"Of course." Her calm is amazing. "He needed a substitute home, after you drove him out of yours. Not that I'll put him up forever. If you hadn't come to me, I would have come to you. I'm ready to hand this burden back."

There's a tremendous boom and the ceiling lights flicker. "Gracious." She swings her chair completely around to her office window, showing me the back of her head. The storm I've been expecting has broken. Rain is smashing at the glass.

"You better hand it back fast," I tell her. "You could lose your job. Stuff like that with students."

She turns to me. "The truth at last. You're here to threaten me." She doesn't look worried.

I tell her I went to Stratford High with Dominic Virgilio. Now he's on the Community Colleges Governing Board. She just smiles. "*I* know Dom Virgilio."

"We'll see who knows him better," I say, though he wouldn't even remember who I was.

"You should be grateful to me," she says. "Very few would trouble themselves to help a boy who's lost his psychic way. And don't think it hasn't cost me, my time has value. I'm a woman who treasures her privacy. Don't think this has given me *any pleasure at all.*"

Phony or real? She looks as if she needs to cry, her face twisting to shut the valve. "Just go away," she tells me.

So I go. It's that or grab her by the throat. I think it's true, she'll send him home: he's disappointed her and hurt her, the same as he's done to us. In the lobby, looking out at the rain, is the sign man. He smiles and offers a pamphlet. "Thanks," I say, patting my breast pocket, "I have one." Which I feel against my chest as I run, zigzagging through the parked cars, raindrops smashing hoods and roofs and shattering like shrapnel. I feel them under my skin, those photographs of an operation, as though doctors are splitting me open already to discipline my dreaming heart.

MORTAL STATE

The Mating Sign

After observing many matings, Gary (1963) gives the following description of this event: The drone alights on the back of the abdomen of the queen, grasping her with all six legs, his head extending over the thorax. The abdomen of the drone curls downward until it contacts the tip of the queen abdomen. If the queen opens her sting chamber, the penis everts and ejaculation occurs very rapidly. If the queen fails to open, the drone may remain in this position for several seconds or until another drone knocks him off. As soon as ejaculation occurs, the instantly paralyzed drone releases from the queen and topples over backwards, and 2 to 3 seconds later a distinct "pop" is heard as the two separate. . . . Gary observed a tethered queen that mated 11 times in quick succession. After everting the penis, the paralyzed drones eventually die, often taking more than an hour.

* * *

When the queen returns from a mating flight she is continuously followed by the excited workers which touch her and lick her "mating sign" (remains of part of the penis of the last drone to mate with her and the coagulated mucus), or may pull it out with their mandibles. . . . Before the second and subsequent matings, the mating sign is removed from the sting chamber of the queen by being attached to the base of the penis of the next drone. At these successive matings the sting chamber of the virgin remains open. Only at the last mating does the queen close the chamber, thus cutting off the bulb of the penis, and returns to the hive with a mating sign.

—The Hive and the Honey Bee

TEN

This scene was in monochrome. Virginia stood at the door in her gray suit. In black jeans, gray sweater, he faced her. Eyes gray in their white faces. She had a long drive, she said. She was meeting a childhood friend for Thanksgiving dinner at a restaurant. "Are you going to your parents' house? You should."

"I might."

"Because I can drop you there. Listen to me. Close the circle." She'd been after him for days. "Leaving is pointless if you never return."

"I'll take the bus if I go."

"I don't think you're going, and I think that's a big mistake."

The camera zoomed in tight. She put a hand on her hip, tilted her head to one side. She'd done her best, her posture said, but who could argue with a—

"If you do go out," she told him, "walk Sally first. And remember to lock up behind you." After a moment's hesitation, as though he were a bug it might not be endurable to squash with a bare hand, she leaned forward—he didn't breathe—and kissed him on the cheek. Then the monitor showed her vanishing behind the gray door. Eli exhaled, wiped his mouth and nose, and turned his face toward the camera.

In the weeks since coming here from Cyril's, he'd felt best on his back—in bed or on this lumpy sofa, reading. Astronomy, cosmogony. Space and matter, anti-matter and time, left him double-jointed, snaking through black holes, from universe to counter-universe. Some days he'd walk the dog, and some nights Virginia would drive him to a shopping mall for, she said, a normalcy booster. Eli liked that. They'd walk past luggage stores—she'd relate her trips to Italy and Greece and Egypt—past jewelry stores—she told him where opals were mined. A sporting-goods store displayed tents and sleeping bags, and she'd talk about *Homo erectus*, summoned from unconsciousness to savagery, inventing society and religion and art because life was so important then. At the end they'd go for Chinese food or she'd even talk him into a movie. Yet now he felt as though he'd never left these yellowish walls, window shades limp on exhausted springs, carpet brindled with stains from Sally's urine.

The telephone rang and he watched until it stopped. His father had been calling, though he never answered, and never took the receiver from Virginia, no matter how angrily she held it toward him, shaking it and mouthing words. Then last week a letter had come—an actual invitation. *Even one day together would be something to be thankful for.*

Well, it would. He felt that too. Nevertheless he'd found that letter unbearably sad.

VV failed, she said, failed utterly, to understand him.

She said his software was bizarre, and she didn't have time to write the manual. When she took her bubble bath, she still liked him there to refill her wine glass, sitting on the closed toilet, listening to her talk, and liked him afterward to massage her in ways that she closed her eyes to describe. Yet she told him all this had to stop, custodial relationships didn't interest her. Once she'd been married to an artist, but wouldn't praise his schlockwork just to protect his male ego. Her intelligence prevented her from cementing a relationship with a man. She was an intuitive genius, the best mind on campus by far, and her colleagues, virtually all, were highly jealous. She told Eli these things from under white drifts of bubbles, or nights when she pushed aside the chessboard, poured wine for them both, and lay with her head in his lap.

Whenever she spoke of Cyril, Eli felt again that they must have had an affair. But now she called him an intellectual primitive, programmed for dominance, sincere and naive. The group had been her idea, not his. They'd planned it as a seminar, to be led by her—she was the one with the qualifications—and then he'd taken it over, as he did everything. She'd end the evening enraged, crying, spilling wine on the carpet, disgusting Eli by falling suddenly asleep, body unwashed and teeth not brushed, helpless in her sweated clothes.

The monitor showed him crossing the room and clicking off the television set, where the Thanksgiving Day parade had been passing, audio set at zero. He stood watching the blank screen. She'd never seen, not once, the connection between them, deeper than this life, the way underground water fed plants that were nothing alike. That he'd come to her from Cyril, who found connections everywhere, was grotesque. Yet how could you be sorry for anything you did, for anything that happened—for how the world worked? A flower didn't choose when it bloomed. On hot days glaciers fed lakes. Death's moment came to every creature. It was all one vast machine of intersecting cogs, reciprocating shafts, teeth engaging teeth, and events were just design displayed in time.

He returned to the sofa. Behind it, Sally was grunting in her sleep. Living with a dog—the choking stink when you came in, bowls of shit-like food spilling onto newspapers—made Eli dream of Cyril's tidy apartment. So did the mess a woman made, tampon cylinders under the furniture, hairs everywhere, the sink and tub, the bedding. At night, lying beside her, he thought of her dark hairs loosening.

What he must do sickened him, but he recognized this sickness. It was a counterweight, part of the mechanism, the big machine. Though he'd forgotten the number, his fingers remembered a pattern of stretches and pressures.

The voice that said hello surprised him, slightly unfamiliar. "Eli?" As if he'd been training it, ever since Eli left, teaching it to vibrate with a beauty that he meant for Eli's inheritance. "Is that you?" The new voice was full, but confidentially soft.

"Hi," he said, "Dad."

"We're all fine," said his father. "And you?"

He said he was fine.

"Mom's fine." Eli knew she was right there, his father had waved her close to listen. He imagined them standing together in the kitchen, his father's free hand grasping the back of his neck as he tried to collect his thoughts. Eli said he'd see them in a little while.

"That's wonderful." His father's new voice burnished the word. "We're going out now to the Stratford-Milford game. Want us to pick you up? Later we'll come back here for dinner." Eli knew that next his father would recite the menu, and pictured him closing his eyes to concentrate. "Sweet potatoes with marshmallow. String beans with almonds and mushrooms." *Cranberry gelatin mold,* said his mother's voice. "And cranberry Jell-O. Apple pie and coconut custard." Eli imagined the meal in progress, a gravy-stained tablecloth, spilling stuffing, the accumulating bones. "Your Uncle Woody'll be here, and your Aunt Violet," his father said, as though Eli might need to be reminded of those relationships. "And your cousin Pal. Ready to be picked up?" His father had become sly.

"No, that's okay. There are some things I have to do. I'll meet you home. I'll come on the bus."

Behind the sofa, Sally snorted. Sometimes he felt that no instrument would be necessary—you could end someone, disorganize him, simply by seeing him honestly, seeing him as circumstance, as elements in flux. Nevertheless he'd practiced. As the dog slept, wheezing, her lower lip fallen away from her slavering teeth, dreams twitching her paws, he'd held the point of a kitchen knife to different parts of her body. Once, by accident, he'd pricked her, drawing a dark drop and making her snort awake to lick the spot.

The whale lay in his opened hand until Eli decided not to take it. But as he gulped orange soda—chilly from the fridge—fizzless, because VV would open cans for just one sip—he stared at the ceiling, and when he looked down again his spread palm was empty. After searching the filthy floor on knees and elbows he guessed the capsule was inside him. It didn't matter; acts were effortless anyway. It was the attitude that was hard. Detachment: a word so naive that Eli pitied anyone who used it, pitied the word itself. He brushed dust from his sleeves and trouser legs, then washed his hands, wishing he could tell Cyril what he was going to do. The urge came from weakness, he knew. But weakness was a thing too. There could be nothing wrong with weakness, any more than there was with apples or snow.

First he'd promised to walk Sally. Eli made his hand reach back and haul her from behind the sofa. She stood, panting quietly, while he snapped her leash onto her flea collar. Outside, she squatted above a patch of dying lawn. He looked away, hearing her splash. Then he led her back into the apartment, where she sniffed out a spot on the carpet and squatted again.

His hand was on the doorknob when he thought of changing into something (as his mother would have said) a little more appropriate. Virginia had bought him some clothes. The store she'd chosen was a cheap one, and although he'd done the best he could—the tie, at least, wasn't bad—he wished her closet door opened into his closet at home, where his trousers still hung expectant, upside-down with creases straight, loyal in their stopped parade, and his jackets were ready on bowed hangers, each hugging the shoulders of the next, patient as though they awaited him unborn.

• • •

The bus took a long time coming—he'd forgotten the holiday schedule—and then he had another wait to transfer. Someone was depressing piano pedals. That was how things were starting to sound. His hands felt warm and thick. He rode the second bus with closed eyes, to its last stop at Armando's Pizza Bar. Beyond the empty parking lot, the beach lay huge at low tide.

He thought he heard, far out on the water, music. But it became clearer the closer he got to Cyril's. When he climbed the porch steps he knew it was coming from inside—shrieking brass and thumping drums that made him feel he could march straight through the solid door. Though nobody answered his knock, Cyril had to be home. His car was right in front.

When Eli had moved out, he'd given back his key to the apartment. Somehow he knew—he couldn't remember ever being told—that Cyril kept a spare in the car. But the car doors were locked too. He climbed back up the porch steps and banged on the door. The band played louder, and now Eli began to think that something must have happened inside, something he didn't want to discover.

Then it came into his head that there was also a spare key for the car. The Thunderbird was slung low. Half underneath it, he despaired—its skinless belly was riddled with likely recesses. He lay still, trying to picture Cyril placing the key, trying to travel back on the astral plane and watch him do it.

And he did see something—Cyril, the Bull, crouched beside the car—a man his size could never slide under. Eli stood, feeling his arms and chest swell, his legs take on Cyril's swagger. This time he just walked around the car, dangling one patting hand, and found the magnetic container clinging inside a fender. When he tugged it free, the keys inside rattled.

An inch open, the front door stopped. He remembered the brass chain. A trumpet fanfare rushed out through the crack and, under the trumpets, a peculiar whimper. Picturing Cyril dead in the bathtub, Eli started to cry, shoving at the door, drawing back and smashing forward, until the screws pulled from the wood and he stood, rubbing his shoulder, in a dim clatter of falling hardware. Now the whimper sounded like a dog.

The drums made him want to stamp. But he tiptoed up the stairs, back through the living room, past the kitchen, to Cyril's bedroom. Through the doorway he could see light flickering against the drawn shades. On the television screen, bands were passing in parade. The music was there. Like festive gods, the huge balloon heads of cartoon animals swayed above a packed avenue.

They were asleep. Eli felt no surprise. Softly he sat on a chair, on top of her carelessly piled clothes. These gears had been designed from the start to engage, these shafts cast to reciprocate. He considered turning down the sound so they wouldn't wake. They were lying wonderfully still. Though he knew both bodies, together they looked peculiar. Like gifts, they wore silk ribbons around their waists—white for the man, the woman's red. A new white puppy crawled out from under the bed. Cyril must have just bought it.

Several bands had played their numbers and marched off the screen before a bolt of horror stiffened him. He should have seen it the second he walked in: both of them were dead.

Why, he screamed silently.

Because they were dangerous.

Well, possibly not.

He knew these voices. They were coming from the television. He barely heard them under the music. To preserve security, they spoke in the rhythm of the march.

But we couldn't take a chance, the President said. *It wasn't an easy decision. As an American, you understand.*

Simply too dangerous, said the Director.

Runs counter to all our traditions, the President said.

There was a chance, one in a billion, said the Director, *that he could do what he was talking about.*

Not politically easy either.

Doomsday scenario.

Many thought he did have the secret of immortality.

The death of the world.

They wanted it for themselves. Their children.

We had to, the Director said. *Can you understand that now?*

Believe me, the President said, *we know how hard this is for you personally.*

Eli nodded, sadder than he had ever felt in his life. They were right. He could feel himself led home, shamed and comforted, by their wisdom and calm.

Then Cyril moved. So did VV. Eli saw her thin hand reach out to a bedside table, pick up a wristwatch, bring it close to her eyes, and put it down again. The music had stopped, the melody: just drums pounded the cadence. The President's voice matched the drumbeat so only Eli would understand. *You, know, your, du, ty, now.* There was pain in that murmur, and a thrilling love.

Stepping in rhythm, he tiptoed out to the kitchen.

Cyril's good knife lay on the cutting board, but it was unclean, fouled with cheese rinds, the seeded gore of tomatoes. From the pegboard where it hung against its painted silhouette, he lifted down the hammer. He tiptoed back, around to Cyril's side of the bed, and, just as VV sat up with a gasp, grabbing the sheet to her breasts, he brought the hammer down on Cyril's temple.

VV was shrieking. Cyril groaned and rolled onto the floor, thrashing half under the bed. In a moment he pulled out something that reminded Eli of grade school: a blade, comically gigantic, but now crippled and sad, missing its wooden block cross-hatched with measuring lines. Only the best students had been allowed to lean above it, cutting paper with a slow grating crunch. Cyril rose on one knee, drawing back the blade, blood running down his face, and Eli hammered him again. The Bull fell sleepily on his side, next to the puppy's wicker basket half-filled with shredded newspaper. His cheeks looked swollen. Eli remembered that he was having dental work: VV had said he was going through hell, and it showed. He aimed away from Cyril's jaw, at a spot behind his eye. With each blow the eyeball rolled in its socket distrustfully, glancing quickly toward him and then away.

The music had begun again. Giant balloons bobbed across the screen, making the walls dance in the shifting light. He covered Cyril with a bed sheet. Where he'd gripped the hammer, his fingers felt crisped. He saw an open oven door, and someone's hands sliding out an oozing glowing body onto a platter.

VV was gone. Eli looked under the bed. Her clothes still lay in a pile, but he couldn't find her in any of the rooms. Then, as he was washing the hammer at the kitchen sink, he heard a noise and stepped into the hall in time to meet her. She seemed to lean toward him, the way she did when she was teaching; there was a lesson in this. But as he waited for her to speak, she turned and ran, leaped, stumbled, banging the walls, naked down the stairs. He winced, imagining her bruised body tonight when she stepped out of her bath, the white bubbles sliding off her shoulders, caught in the hair at her center.

Eli dried the hammer and returned it to its pegboard silhouette. With one hand against each wall, the stairs were simple. But on the sidewalk, he planned where his feet would go—he felt like a reconnaissance aircraft guiding infantry—until he reached the bus stop at Armando's Pizza Bar and sank onto the bench.

Up the block, in front of Cyril's, three police cars had appeared. Eli saw the officers go inside, one of them pulled by a wildly barking dog. A bus paused in front of him with a mechanical sigh, then left when he didn't move. The police were going from house to house. Virginia stood on the sidewalk, wearing somebody else's bathrobe, and was driven away. No longer feeling the bench beneath him, Eli lounged on a throne of air. An ambulance arrived, and he held his breath as two men carried out something long.

Finally the last police car cruised right past him. In half a block it stopped, backed up. A cop got out and looked at Eli, fists on hips, head cocked, like a man finding scratches on his fender, or dog mess on his lawn. "What're you doing?" His partner was watching from the car window.

"Waiting for the bus." In jacket and tie, he felt safe.

But he knew his voice sounded funny.

The cop nodded, staring at him. "You're stoned," he said. "Let's see what you've got in your pockets."

Eli obediently emptied them, and the cop nodded again when there were no drugs. "Go on home," he said, getting back in his car. "You're high as King Kong's tits."

Light was different, now—it struck things from the side. In the gutter glittered a beer can, violently cleft and folded. Its shape reminded him of something: the place where VV's body met her legs. As the glowing can was extinguished, the air grew darker and colder. Eli thought he should get on the next bus; for a long time he'd been hearing water behind him. The tide was coming in.

And now there was another sound, a kind of buzzing. It grew to a roar as a stream of motorcycles appeared. Like muscle-bound men attempting the split, they stretched their front wheels forward on angled forks. Two by two, they turned into Armando's parking lot, slung so low that in profile their drivers looked diagonal, feet thrust forward, bodies cupped in the bowls of seats. Eli could see their jackets. These were the Zombies. He had never known there were so many.

The roaring died. "Closed," someone said. "Fuck it."

"Go to Scotty's," said another voice.

"Fuck him."

"Fuck you."

"Fuck yourself."

They argued, many at once, making an eddy in Eli's ears. Bottles were passed, the riders still straddling their machines. He heard the smash of glass. Someone yelled, "Hey, cunt!"

"You asshole. It's a guy."

"It's a cunt."

"Ask him."

"Hey, cunt!"

"Answer him, cunt."

They meant him, which was funny. How long had it been since he'd cut his hair? He opened his mouth but couldn't answer, and just smiled.

"He's flying," one of them said.

"No shit."

"Let's take him for a ride."

They came over, some of them, and lifted him into the air. Either he was numb or they were gentle. The smell of them—gasoline, sweat, liquor—was complicated and wonderful. He was lowered onto a seat, his face squashed into a jacket, squeezed breathless by a woman who climbed on behind him, arms and legs hugging with irresistible strength.

Then they blasted away, at a speed that instantly seemed tremendous. Eli could hardly see. The cold wind filled his eyes with tears. They roared like bombers through the streets, cornering at a lean that made pavement into sky. He felt transformed, his mind no longer his, the way it became in the swimming minutes before sleep. He could hardly remember what he was leaving. The spreading mystery erased every need and purpose. Were the other Zombies behind them in procession, or waiting back at the beach? He thought they'd reached Stratford, now. Something shone like the river. A darker line, set at an angle, was Deer Hill Road—he guessed they were taking him home, but they never slowed. The woman's hands were squeezing his crotch. Maybe for warmth: Eli's own hands were frozen, paralyzed. His ears burned, one so fiercely that maybe she had it in her teeth.

Later they were lifting him off, back at the parking lot. His body was trembling and the roar had made it hard to hear. "He smells like shit."

"He needs a bath."

"Fast," someone yelled from a group that was staying with the motorcycles.

Eli wasn't frightened. All that remained was the lesson he'd always waited for, which would show—if he paid attention despite the pitching of sand and Sound and red sky—who he was. "He's gonna puke," a voice warned, and he felt the ground slam against him. "Shit, he got me." There was laughter. Eli smiled into the sand. They took off his clothes and dragged him down where it was wet. "He's cold," somebody said. A bottle was forced between his lips, and he coughed out fire.

"Don't waste it."

"Then fucking finish it."

"Let him have the bottle up the ass."

He was turned onto his stomach. His legs were parted. They were screwing the neck of the bottle into his rectum. Suddenly it hurt. He thought of VV's theory—hypothesis—and could feel himself surrounded everywhere by Cyril's spores, a whiteout, a snowstorm of immortality. As they twisted deeper he gulped air, swallowing that virus forever.

"There you go," someone said. Before his eyes, buckled boots pressed water from the wet sand. The boots left and the water seeped back, filling the heelprints, melting their walls.

Water bathed his chin. The sand, filling and draining, fizzed, and the waves hissed like someone demanding silence. He thought of his parents' house, where the Thanksgiving meal would now be finished, dishes stacked in the sink. They'd all be in the living room, talking. Spilled food under the table—if he were there he'd have the carpet sweeper out. In his palms, on his fingers, he felt its handle.

As the water licked his face he was washed by circles of color. There was something in his nose: he could hear the bubbling. His nose cleared and the sound went away but returned, now in his chest. The wet sand humped beneath him. Then there was quiet. The rings of color were still coming, swiftly growing darker, and in the center of them—shrinking as he approached, threatening to vanish before he could arrive—the deepest and tightest of black holes.

It was the lady, the woman, the girl Zombie who came to take him home: Eli sprang up to meet her. Before they climbed onto her bike, she wrapped him in a coat of fur. Her speed made him close his eyes until he smelled honey, and felt the crunch of gravel, and heard his father call his name.

E L E V E N

North End, South End—*everyone* went to the game on Thanksgiving morning. There was no reserved seating. But for as many years as Hook could remember, people like the Underwoods had lined the rows up front, squeezed into Stratford High jackets stored the rest of the year in cellophane, while Smalls and such climbed benches until the game shrank below them, to keep each play from mattering more than they could bear.

After he'd spoken to Eli, Hook had feared hanging up, then hated to leave the house. He nearly announced he was staying home, touching his chest to blame his operation: though the stitches were out, his incision still tingled, and he couldn't stop fingering the rectangular lump, like a burial mound, in his shaven chest. But he hadn't missed the Stratford-Milford game since he was ten. And Marigolde would be there—these last weeks he'd hardly seen her. A few times to talk. Only once, the noon of the day before his surgery, to make love.

Wedged between Helen and Woody, hip to hip on a metal plank, he couldn't easily turn and look. Then, when the first quarter ended with Stratford up 6–0, he heard Ken's whoop. There they were, a swarm of Smalls, packed in the highest bleacher seats, with blankets and baskets, cans of beer and cowbells, kids dropping over the top rail to swing down the web of steel in back—Hook could remember doing that—and Marigolde perched next to Ken. He tried to catch her eye. But it was Ken who saw him, shouted, elbowed her and made her sight along his pointing finger, then stood to aim at Hook with something shiny, squeezing out a hoarse metallic bleat: ka-DOO-kah.

In the second quarter, Stratford kept fumbling. Roars of satisfaction, joyous ding-dongs, rolled from the Milford stands across the field. Woody leaped up to shake both fists at the wavering Stratford line—"Dig in, damn you!"—while Violet screamed, "Aggressive! Aggressive!" "Hustle there," Hook called weakly. He loved the game but doubted he should. At the center of the howling, most of the boys seemed thin, lost in their helmets and padded uniforms.

Helen watched quietly, as though the game were one more misfortune she'd been expecting and could endure. Hook knew their marriage was finished. Another child, he'd told her each day and each night, would be absolutely— But all she ever said was *go*. Leave if you want. And beyond that challenge, Hook couldn't think. Too many feelings had blinked out, the way a magician tapped and presto-ed glasses of blood to water. At the end of panic or passion, when every emotion toppled into the next, came one like a blank domino.

Half time. The bands marched onto the field. First Milford, advancing in quickstep with a crisp drum roll and waves of high-jabbing knees. Helen wanted to go to the bathroom so Hook swiveled to let her by. But the second she stood, she clutched his shoulder and sank back down. "Sorry," she said. When she rose again she seemed fine.

Hook said, "I'll go with you." As they descended the grandstand, Helen reached for him. Her fingers felt like something thawing: chilly, stiff, moist. Hook couldn't remember when they'd last held hands. At the toilets, there was a line. Though he'd never known her to faint, this morning she'd said she thought she might. He imagined her passed out on the trampled grass, amid candy wrappers and spilled popcorn. "I'll wait," he said.

"I'd rather you got me a Coke."

Hook eyed the line in front of her. Then he took off, cutting toward the refreshment trailer. Under the grandstand the grass was rank. From there, all he saw of the crowd seated above him were their feet severed at the ankle, cheap utilitarian parts, like secondhand items flung onto shelves to be sold. He picked a path past proud mounds of dog manure, neat cylinders of it and trodden smears, as screaming children overhead thundered up and down the stands. Hook stopped still, closed his eyes against the stink and clamor, and thought of grace. Cleverer men, he believed, outgrew these longings. He guessed it was Eli's fault that he couldn't. If you had a kid you felt some hope for, then you surrendered some for yourself. Hope had to go somewhere. It couldn't be destroyed, it could only be scattered, like quicksilver from a snapped thermometer.

Coming back with Helen's drink, he had to squeeze through a mob. Children were running everywhere.

There was Pal with a cigarette, tall among his friends, shaven head bobbing. Now he was seeing a psychiatrist. He was down to two courses but hanging on in school. The kid, Woody had explained, had passed the crisis. He'd finish out this miserable college, probably transfer somewhere bigger. Someday be a human being. Though Hook knew he should feel glad, the injustice of Pal's redemption, with only his Eli left behind, broke his heart. Sometimes it happened with bees—one didn't grow wings, another never developed the jaws to cut free from its capped cell—and every South End family had spawned miscarriage, monstrous birth, early death. But when you had only one child, his insistent withering, no matter what you did, was agony. The sight of Pal made Hook want to turn and start running. He imagined a place where he wouldn't recognize a single person or object. The air, the light, would have no memory.

He found Helen still waiting in a line that seemed impossibly long. And there next to her, chatting and laughing, was Marigolde. Just two girl friends waiting for the ladies' room.

"So," Marigolde greeted him.

Hook wiped his shoes on the grass. He could feel himself again beginning to hope, though it hurt like flexing an injured limb. The Stratford band was playing. He heard the slow brass strains, the grave drum thump, of his high school anthem.

Time ne'er will plun-der
(boom, boom)
The mem'ries we hold
(boom, boom, boom, boom)

Oh Al-ma Ma-ter
(boom, boom)
Oh crim-son and gold

Helen closed her eyes. Her forehead looked sprayed with an atomizer. Her posture was rigid, chin lifted as if to hear the music better.

"Oh crimson, oh gold," Marigolde sang, smiling at him.

"Help me," Hook said. "Help her. Let's get her," he pointed under the grandstand, "over there. She has to get off her feet."

First Marigolde seemed puzzled, half smiling, blinking rigid black lashes. Then he saw her understand. "She's going to have—"

He nodded. He was surprised how easy it was to nod, like signing an unread contract. But on Marigolde's face the terms were clear: they were lost to each other. For this final gift of despair, Hook loved her freshly. Yet he could also see her face later today, at her parents' house, where the Smalls would gather for Thanksgiving dinner, as she recited his betrayal—how he'd sworn he'd return, never mentioned a baby—surrounded by her family, perspiring in their hugs, while Ken, looking fierce, brought her beer after beer.

Like royalty, Helen walked between them. "Well," Marigolde said, "congratulations." Helen smiled tightly, no lips, eyes closed. They found a clear space and sat on the grass while the old song rolled.

Wave thy ban-ner
For-eeeeee-ver

(boom, boom)
Oh Strat-ford High

Marigolde was crying. So, to his amazement, was Helen. Hook felt like a juggler of knives, already up to his limit, who'd been tossed one more. And he was going to handle it, make it join the arch overhead, with something not very far from grace. If his hands were bloody, grace cost that—it was a joy but no pleasure. How could they ever be clean unless he let everything drop?

He wished he could hold both women. But they seemed farther away than Eli. Hook began to search the crowd: lately he'd found himself expecting his son, watching for his approach in the distance. As he tended his hives, narrowing their entrances to keep out mice, drilling top holes in case of deep snow, he'd imagined Eli beside him, holding the smoker. Again and again, finishing his year's labor, he'd looked up quickly. In the early dark, rather than return to the house, he'd worked at his last tasks more and more slowly—feeling his need thicken, like a muscle trying to contract—until now there was nothing he could do but leave his bees to wait out the cold.

When they reached home, Hook thought he was starving. Soon the house was aromatic as ampules snapped under his nose. Woody poured the Scotch while Pal took two cans of beer upstairs to listen to music in Eli's room. It frightened Hook to imagine him up there, sprawled on Eli's bed, his head on Eli's pillow, a beer balanced on his bony chest.

In the kitchen there was a conversation Hook couldn't hear, but didn't need to. Violet came out, pulling Helen by the waist—"Is it *true?*"—and grinning wildly. "Jerry, you *devil.*" She threw herself on him.

Woody stared at Helen, who was blushing, a thing Hook had never seen. "I don't believe this. No," Woody said, putting his arms around his sister. Then he punched Hook on the shoulder and began to laugh.

Hook felt the jollity expand and thin as though it knew that space must not be empty, but nobody mentioned Eli. Hook had left the house unlocked—Eli might have lost his key—and had looked in every room when they came in. Now he remembered he hadn't told Marigolde, and wanted to phone her quickly, while it might still be true: listen, he's on his way, it's all worked out, that was a joke at half time! But even then, as they were changing goals on the field, Hook had felt within his life the same inexorable turn.

When, after another hour, Eli still hadn't come, he started to feel sad and drunkenly wise. To keep himself from watching at the window, he lay on the sofa, letting Woody keep their glasses full. Later, Helen called him to help lift the turkey from the oven. Hook gave her a look of fellow-suffering, which she wouldn't meet. Right now, he felt, was when they'd put their arms around each other, just stand like that awhile. But Violet was there, and he returned to the sofa. Woody—who thirty-one years ago had played in the Stratford-Milford game himself—was explaining something about the fourth quarter, his forefingers sewing patterns into the air. Pal came down, hungry. He cracked some walnuts and went back upstairs with another beer.

An hour more and they began the meal. The low sun filled the room. They ate in silence, Hook stuffing himself as urgently as though he were packing a wound. But what had happened to his stomach? He'd eaten three times this much, back when he and Marigolde had celebrated Thanksgiving with the Smalls. Bursting, he stood at a living-room window, uncinching his belt. Two fingers slid between his shirt buttons, touching softly below his collarbone. When the theatrical surgeon had first held the thing up in his gloved hand, Hook had thought it was a cigarette lighter, and he'd grinned, feeling silly, while they were slitting a pocket in him.

Shadows were spreading. He saw how they rushed down western slopes to fill the bottoms of depressions, crept up the eastern sides. He told Woody, "Mangiacapra wants this land, but I'm not selling."

"He claimed you were," Woody said, "and I told him he was wrong. Will you quit worrying?" He laid an arm across Hook's shoulders. Woody was sweating, shirt soaked halfway to his belt, and the male smell promised normalcy. "Your boy got stuck somewhere. Okay?"

"I'm not so worried."

"Pretty soon he'll call and say come get me."

"He wanted to come," Hook said, sliding both hands under his waistband to soothe his belly. "That's what counts." He watched darkness climb the trees until only their crowns floated in light.

When tires crunched on the gravel, he looked up at Helen's eyes. "Must have gotten a ride," he said, and Woody said, "Told you."

Hook stood, then sat. "Everyone just act normal."

"I'll fix him a plate." Helen grabbed, from the setting in front of Eli's old chair, the one clean plate left on the table. Somebody was climbing the porch steps. Someone heavy: Eli with suitcases, Eli stamping in rage.

And when Hook opened the door it seemed like magic. His son was transformed—made tall and broad, small-headed and long-haired, fitted with a uniform, armed with a holstered pistol. Pinhead's face left no hope. "Your boy here?" He was looking past them, around the room, toward the staircase.

"We're expecting him," Helen said. "What—"

Pinhead glanced out a window, as though Eli might be approaching now. Hook looked too. "I don't know," Pinhead said, "but the Cyril guy, Jimmy Birmingham, he's dead."

To Hook it made no sense. Pinhead was talking about forcible entry, blunt instruments, and Pal was swinging at the air and saying the cops had done it—this was just what Cyril had expected! Exactly what he'd predicted! The scar at Pal's hairline grew bright red. But then he stopped himself. He grabbed his head with both hands. And Hook saw him become different, change the way Woody had said, as though someone his opposite, someone like Eli, were entering him. He asked when it had happened, whether there were witnesses.

"I better talk to your kid," Pinhead told Hook apologetically.

Helen had her arms around his chest. Hook realized that he'd begun to bend over, hugging himself like a tramp in winter. He straightened. "Eli didn't do it."

Pinhead was moving from window to window, closing

Venetian blinds. "Maybe you want to call your family lawyer. It's advisable."

"No. I can find him." Saying this, Hook felt relief, the return of savage hope.

"He could be in a state of mind where you better not get close."

Woody said, "We'll take two cars. Pal will ride with me. Pinhead, don't hurt him if he comes."

"Don't worry," Hook told Helen, "it'll be okay."

From the hall closet she brought him a red nylon shell, Eli's windbreaker. Then, gracefully but suddenly, she sat down, her mouth surprised.

"Don't," Hook said, when she started to push herself back up. She gripped the arms of her chair, frowning but not resisting, as he crouched to pull off her shoes. On his knees he hugged her, and she held his head between her breasts, her heart beating aloud.

Outside, the last cold light was draining into the earth. Hook hurried to his car, past his silent nursery hives, their colonies tightly clasped in winter cluster. All the bees were now one life.

From the North End through Paradise Green to Stratford Center they sped, up the West Broad Street ramp and onto the Connecticut Turnpike, Woody and Pal leading in the Cadillac, Hook pursuing. Each sweep of approaching lights outlined their heads in the rear window. Motel billboards were lighting up as they drove past, and brilliant signs named dark factories. From the pillared height where they raced above Bridgeport, the west was still irradiated by the buried day. They exited heading south. Near Seaside Park, Woody pulled over sharply, and Pal came running back. They'd stopped in front of Cyril's.

Every window was dark. "We'll split up," Hook decided. "Which way would he go?"

Pal shrugged. Then he pointed toward a bar at the end of the street, its neon light flickering across an empty parking lot, and beyond that the sand: red, black, red. "There, maybe."

Hook said, "It looks closed."

It was closed. They separated and began to search. The streets were almost empty. Hook pulled the Beetle nearly onto the sidewalk each time he saw someone, though he already knew by shape or gait that it wasn't Eli. It had been months, maybe he'd changed—suddenly it was hard to see his face. Hook worked through the grid of streets, from the turnpike south to the water, from the park west to the dump. Each time he passed the Caddy he looked to see if a third person was inside, and Woody and Pal peered back at him.

They met again at the bar, window to window in the parking lot, and shut off their engines. Hook heard the lapping of water on wet sand. He couldn't guess how long they'd been searching. Outside the bar was a pay phone. He called his house and Pinhead answered: no word yet. "You better come home," he said.

When Hook returned to the cars, Woody took his arm. "I don't think it's any use, Red."

"Sure it is. It's getting light." Hook pointed over the water to the rising moon, huge and accessible at the end of a silver path.

"Okay, let's be logical," Pal said. "Where would he

go. After he did this, where would he go, what would he do."

Then Hook raised his eyes and saw, lying in the waves' lap, what might be the breast of a sandbar. Woody and Pal looked too, and they were all in a wallowing run across the beach, feet plunging and rising in falling veils of sand, mud, water. When Hook saw what it was—not changed after all, only soaked and limp as stewed meat—something in him shriveled and he lost a connection with his legs. It was Pal who splashed ahead to reach it first, lifted it with surprising strength, and carried it up the beach.

Woody seized the body, held it upside down. Water drained out, an astonishing volume. He laid it on its back. Then he reached up, grabbed Hook's head, and pulled it toward the sand until one eye pressed a cold eye. Woody began to pump the breastbone, leaning his weight onto his forearms. "Breathe," he said.

Hook fitted his lips to Eli's—colder than earth, frigid as the parts he'd yanked from the cavity of the frozen turkey. With both hands, he molded the limp jaw and cheeks to seal their mouths. On the first breath he was soaked as icy water spewed from Eli's nostrils. Then came bubbling. Hook pinched the nostrils and saw his son's chest rise and fall as he breathed into him.

He heard Woody tell Pal, "Go call an ambulance. You got quarters?" The waves were seething. Woody grunted as he thrust. Each time Hook took his mouth from Eli's, his own warm breath sighed back up in his face.

He heard the siren, but not the feet coming across the

sand, and when they pulled him off he didn't know why he was the one they were wrapping in a blanket. "You're okay," a man said, holding his wrist. They'd wrapped Pal and Woody, too. It seemed cruel for Eli to be strapped to a stretcher, out in such cold.

They walked back to the flickering parking lot. Hook saw them slide Eli into the ambulance, featureless beneath a sheet, unformed as he'd been before his birth. That was the change the sea had worked. Hook started to free himself from the blanket. "For God's sake," the orderly told him, "keep it on you."

Pal said from within his blanket, "Ride with Dad. I'll drive yours."

"No," Hook said, "I'm all right." He knew hope was never lost, he knew it always went somewhere. His heart could not refuse to beat. The machine would make it beat. Its chambers would pulse, his blood would hurry, his brain would be suffused with knowing, every atom of him with grace. Still wrapped in the blanket, he got into his car, his shoes grinding sand against the floor mat and pedals. Eli's red jacket lay on the seat beside him like the leavings of a metamorphosis. He pumped the accelerator twice and turned the key—she churned, she shook, unwilling to come to life. Then she did, and Hook's lights split the dark.

Chapter One originally appeared in *Indiana Review* and Chapter Three originally appeared in *Formations*.

Santa Fe Public Library